BATTLE EARTH IX

NICK S. THOMAS

© 2013 Nick S. Thomas

The right of Nick S. Thomas to be identified as the Author of the Work has been asserted by him in accordance with the Copyright, Designs and Patents Act 1988.

First published in the United Kingdom by Swordworks Books.

ISBN 978-1-911092-13-1

Typeset by Swordworks Books
Printed and bound in the UK & US
A catalogue record of this book is available
from the British Library

Cover design by Swordworks Books
www.swordworks.co.uk

BATTLE EARTH IX

NICK S. THOMAS

PROLOGUE

The outbreak of war on Earth between human adversaries shocked the foundations of the alliance of nations that had fought so desperately to keep Earth free and the human race alive.

Mechs now serve openly beside humans in the UEN armies, and the use of clones is a poorly guarded secret that came to light too late to make a difference. When the forces of the UEN took control of the Earth Defence Grid, with the intention of turning it on Earth cities, it became clear that peace was no longer an option.

Taylor was the man for the job, to save Earth from the devastation of its own weapons, but he had a choice - save his friends or save the planet. Unable to let his friends die, he compromised and destroyed Earth's defences in the process of making them all safe. Taylor only ever had the best intentions, but has his unwavering loyalty to his friends put Earth in the greatest danger it has ever faced?

CHAPTER ONE

Taylor's eyes opened slowly, but he couldn't see much at all. His sight was blurred, and his head was pounding. He could just about hear an occasional drone that sounded like metal on metal. He could taste his own blood, which was never a good sign, and the air was stale. A face appeared before him, and even though he could not see clearly, the outline was enough to tell him it was Eli.

For a moment, he had no recollection of where they were or why, but as he looked around and saw the body of the ship's XO strewn across the bridge, it began to come back to him. Parker had still not said a word as she looked at him in amazement. She finally turned to someone else beside her.

"He's awake!"

A huge figure stepped up and loomed over her. It was Jafar. He reached down and hauled Taylor to his feet, without checking to see if he was injured. His back clicked and his joints crunched as he was hauled upright, but he had no choice other than stand on his own two feet. He shook his head at the lack of finesse, and it too clicked as it loosened up.

"How are you feeling?"

"Like shit, Parker."

"Can nothing really kill you?" Herbert asked him.

Taylor looked over at the Sergeant. He had a bandage wrapped around his head and covering his left eye, yet seemed unbothered by his injuries.

"I wouldn't be so sure."

His sight was coming back as was his hearing, and yet the pounding of metal on metal had not stopped. Every impact felt like a hammer to his aching head.

"What in hell is that god awful pounding?" he asked.

Parker's face turned from the relief and hope from when he had awoken to despair and fear.

"What is it?"

He looked to Jafar for answers, knowing the alien would give him a straight response.

"The remained Mechs aboard are sweeping the ship and eliminating all humans."

"All? The crew as well?"

"As far as we can tell, yeah."

"So the wolves are at our door?"

"That about sums it up, Sir," Herbert replied.

"Any word from Jones?"

"He survived the crash but no idea now. Last contact, he was going radio silent with hostiles nearby."

Taylor looked around to see what assets they had at their disposal. A dozen of them were still on their feet. Several others lay dead, and three were conscious but unable to walk. The survivors of the bridge crew were huddled in one corner and under guard by one of his own. As he tried to think, the banging on the door interfered with his every thought.

"What do we do?" asked Parker.

"Make that goddamn noise stop!" he yelled.

"You want to open the door? We have no idea how many are out there. They've been hitting it with everything they've got for the last ten minutes, to no avail. We're safe in here."

"On a sinking ship?"

The thought hadn't crossed her mind. The wave of Mechs beating at the door had been the focus of their attention. Taylor strode over to the prisoners. They looked just as terrified as Parker did when he first awoke.

"Those aliens want to rip everyone of us apart, you can see that, right?"

They nodded cautiously.

"This war is human versus alien, always has been. You can either stand with us and fight your way out of here, or die at their hands. When we get clear, you can stay with us, or hand yourselves in as POWs, but right now you have a choice. What'll it be?"

"We'll fight," said one of them, without hesitation.

"Release them, and get whatever weapons and ammo you can."

His own people looked uneasy with the situation, but they dared not oppose him.

"We're gonna get ourselves out of this heap, if we have to rip it apart with our bare hands."

* * *

"Run!" Jones shouted.

Gunfire struck the ceiling above him, and a panel smashed down over his head, but he kept moving.

"Where the hell are we going, Captain?" Herrera called out, breathlessly.

"I got no idea, away from them!"

They passed a few Navy crew, who did not even notice who they were, but as they reached an intersection ahead, Jones was brought to an abrupt halt when he almost fell over a line of German Marines. They raised their weapons at each other, but neither fired - it was a standoff. No one said a word as they tried to work out what to do. They heard gunfire off to their flank, Jones and Herrera turned ever so slightly to look. Twenty metres down, Mechs were stomping on past at another intersection, and bodies were dropping around them.

"You see that?" Jones asked the man at the front, "They're killing every human they find. It's us against them now."

The German didn't respond. Jones could see he was a Sergeant called Lang, but he looked newly promoted and was young for the rank. Charlie doubted the man had ever seen combat until that day. He lowered his own rifle, revealing Taylor's nametag. It immediately caught the man's eye. It was a lie to continue on in the persona of the Colonel, but he wasn't going to forgo any advantage he had.

"I don't want to fight you, Sergeant. That's the enemy, right there. They are the ones tearing your friends apart. Come with me, and let's get out of here together."

The Sergeant looked back to his men. None of them looked keen on a fight. He slowly turned back and accepted.

"Okay, we will fight beside you."

"All right, where are we right now, and how do we get to the bridge?"

It's a few decks above us, but why would you want to go there? We need to get off this ship."

"I have a few friends to find first. We stick together, and we double our odds of survival, what'll it be?"

The Sergeant accepted once again.

"Lead the way," Jones ordered.

The dozen marines Lang had with him stuck close at his back, as the Sergeant formed up beside Jones. As they began to move, he swamped Jones with questions.

"Is this another invasion? Is this happening all over again? Did we do this? Did we choose the wrong side?"

Jones didn't want to be the bearer of bad news, but he had no answers the Sergeant would want to hear.

"Just focus on what's before us. Whatever happened two minutes ago, two months ago, two years ago, it doesn't matter now. You can see the threat that lies before you. You put in your all, and that's all that matters."

Lang sighed and smiled a little, at least feeling a little relieved he was not being held to blame. Up ahead, five bodies of crewmembers were scattered across the deck. Lang slowed on reaching them, staring wide-eyed at the corpses.

"Nothing you can do for them now," Jones said quietly.

He grabbed the man's arm and dragged him onwards.

"The bridge, Sergeant, lead the way."

Lang didn't say a word, but he did follow the command. Screams rang out from up ahead, and they stopped for just a moment. More crewmembers were rushing towards them and clearly being chased.

"How many Mechs did you have aboard?" asked Jones.

The Sergeant shrugged. It was presumably information beyond his pay grade.

"Must be hundreds of them," said Silva, who had

worked his way up to the front.

How can anyone have ever thought this was a good idea? Jones asked himself, shaking his head.

The fleeing crewmembers reached them but made no attempt to stop. They barrelled past the troops.

"Where are they heading?"

"Same place we should be, Colonel, the lifeboats."

It was a tempting proposition, but he wasn't going to leave Taylor and the rest of the Inter-Allied behind. He prayed they were still alive, but he already knew Mitch would be at least. Lang went to move forward, but Jones grabbed his arm.

"Where are you going?"

"The bridge?"

"Who do you think those crew were running from? Take up position, and be ready to fire."

The Sergeant looked sheepish, but he looked back and gave the signal to his section. The corridor went silent for a moment as they lined the corridor, taking what little cover from the support beams they could. Jones' people used their shields for extra cover. A moment later they heard the heavy footsteps of Mechs stomping towards them. It was an obnoxious noise that still sent shivers down Jones' spine, but he'd learnt to bear it long ago.

"Ready?"

The Sergeant looked terrified, to the extent Jones wondered if he had ever fired his weapon in anger. He

13

knew the answer was probably no.

"When you see them, you remember they're the ones who are killing your comrades, you hear?" he whispered to Lang.

The Sergeant nodded and flicked the safety off his weapon.

Christ! He still had it on, Jones thought.

A second later two Mechs stepped into view with their weapons at the ready. They were completely unaware of the gun line they were running into and had no time to respond. Dozens of shots rang out and riddled the creatures until they dropped down stone dead.

As they hit the deck, more stepped past them, their weapons firing. It was the same relentless advance they had gotten so used to seeing from the alien soldiers. Jones felt a heavy impact be absorbed by his shield, and several other shots smashed the bulkhead around them, but to little effect. Just five Mechs passed over the bodies of the first two and were cut down almost as quickly by the volley of automatic fire. Jones could see a look of almost surprise in Lang's face as the corridor fell silent.

"Come on!" he yelled, as he moved forward, expecting the Sergeant to guide him. When they reached the Mechs, he noticed a slight movement in one and fired a three-shot burst into the creature without breaking stride. Lang almost fell over in surprise as the weapon discharged, but Jones pulled him along, in order to have no further time wasted.

"Elevators are out, so we'll have to take the stairs," said Lang.

"Lead the way."

The Sergeant wanted nothing more than to drop back and let someone else do so, but Jones was adamant he should be at the front. Lang took ten steps, then stopped and looked back at Jones, as if asking 'how much further do I have to do this?' But Jones simply nodded and gestured for him to carry on. They got to the entrance to the next floor. There was no sign of life, just a few screams of either agony or panic in the distance.

"We can't help them," Jones said.

He knew he was asking the Sergeant to leave his people when he wasn't willing to do the same, but the Sergeant complied anyway.

As they turned onto the next stairs, they came to an abrupt halt. They saw a figure on the stairs above them. They quickly raised their weapons ready to shoot, but soon realised it was a marine cowering against the wall. Jones lowered his weapon and stepped up cautiously to the man. He looked terrified and couldn't even bring himself to raise his weapon, simply remaining frozen and sitting on the steps. Jones couldn't see any visible sign of injury.

"You okay, marine?"

He got no response, so he slapped the man's helmet firmly. Life suddenly returned to the man's eyes, and all his attention was turned on Jones.

"You hurt?"

He shook his head.

"Then get your arse up and get in this fight," Jones spoke to him sternly.

He grabbed the marine and hauled him to his feet.

"We're fighting our way off this boat. You want to join us, or stay down there and die?"

His nametag read 'Fuchs', but Taylor could see no sign of rank. He couldn't be older than twenty and had a boyish face that had never known war.

"Fuchs?" Jones asked.

The marine looked down at his uniform and looked confused, but then turned to Lang who he seemed to recognise.

"It's okay, Private. They're with us."

Jones grabbed Fuch's helmet and pulled him round, forcing him to look right at him.

"No time for buggering about, Private. There's a war to fight, and you're slap bang in the middle of it. Now fall in and get to work."

He nodded in response and appeared to right his back, holding himself a little taller and with some pride. Jones could see he had just witnessed the horrors of war he himself had grown all too familiar with, and all he needed were some friends at his side.

"You gonna fall in, Private?" Jones asked.

Confidence returned to his eyes, and he stepped past Jones to take up position with the Sergeant. He looked back to see Silva pointing at his watch.

"How far are we from the bridge?" Jones asked Lang.

"Not far."

That's a big help, he thought, as he pointed for the Sergeant to go on. They carried on cautiously up the last few steps. The sound of the gunfire grew louder.

"It's Taylor, has to be," he muttered.

"Taylor? You're Taylor," replied Lang.

Busted!

"No, I'm not Taylor. The name's Jones, but as far as you're concerned, I might as well be Taylor, who is in there right now and needs our help, you got that?"

He agreed without any hesitation, seeing the unforgiving look in Jones' eyes. Jones didn't need a guide anymore, for he just had to follow the sound of gunfire. He took the last few steps and got out into the corridor. Just as he did, two Mechs rushed into view at a junction up ahead. He fired a snap shot before they disappeared from view. It hit a creature, forcing it to stop and turn quickly to face him, but in doing so presented a perfect target.

Jones quickly raised the weapon for a better aim and fired a burst. Fuchs and Silva quickly joined his side. The creature got off just a single shot that hit the ceiling before it collapsed as a smouldering pile of metal on the deck. The second Mech turned the corner to come back at them, and Jones barely got his shield up in time to take one of the hits and step aside for cover with the others.

Without a word, he pulled a grenade from his waist and armed it. As he launched it, the creature paced out to get them in its sights. Jones dropped to one knee and took shelter behind his shield. It took three shots before the grenade ignited between the feet of the Mech. Chunks of metal were launched across the room, and two large shards of shrapnel impeded in his shield which was now already buckled and weakened in several places.

Silva was up and past before he was on his feet, rushing for the sound of the battle going on just around the corner. As he reached the site of the grenade blast, he opened fire on full auto. Jones took the bend to find seven Mechs with their backs to them, trying to get their way through the open door of the bridge.

Fuchs, Lang and, six others joined them in what felt more like a firing squad. The nine of them held down their triggers until all magazines were empty, and all that remained before them was a heap of metal. Blue blood poured out across the deck from dozens of penetrations of the armoured suits. Jones knew there was someone still alive aboard the bridge; he only hoped it was more than a few. There was utter silence now. Not a cry of pain or a gunshot to be heard.

"Taylor!" Jones shouted.

No response came.

"Colonel Taylor!" he called again.

The worry was starting to really set in as he paced forward towards the door. He took each step more cautiously than the last. He wasn't sure he wanted to see what lay beyond the entrance.

"Jones?" a voice returned.

It was growly and dry. Jones got to the door with his rifle held ready to fire at a moment's notice. There were a number of figures moving, and all of them his comrades. He took a deep breath, lowered his weapon, and stepped firmly through the entrance.

"Jones? You made it."

He looked to see the coarse voice was indeed Taylor. He was sitting propped up against a back wall. His nose was broken, and a deep cut ran from his eyebrow down over his top lip. Most of the survivors around him were wounded in some way, and many others lay dead around them.

"Some rescue attempt, hey?" asked Taylor.

"We're alive, aren't we?"

Taylor looked around at the devastation around them. He was glad to see his closest friends had made it, but so many more of his comrades had not.

"So what's our situation, Mitch?"

"Shit."

Taylor staggered to his feet, noting Jones was still awaiting a proper answer.

"Honestly? Somewhere in the Atlantic, beyond that I have no clue."

"We still on the surface?"

Taylor shrugged. "Your guess is as good as mine."

He turned to the remaining crewmembers.

"Well?"

The pilot stuttered.

"Simple answer!" Jones said.

"In theory, if all breaches were sealed, I guess we could float. But with the damage we took before and during impact, I can't imagine we're too airtight."

"So what are you saying?"

"That we're taking on water," Taylor replied.

"How long do we have?" asked Jones.

The pilot shrugged.

"I suggest we make a move fast. At the bottom of the ocean bed ain't how I saw myself ending," stated Spears.

Rains stepped out from the back of the line and appeared remarkably unscathed by the fighting or crash landing. Taylor looked at him astonished.

"Where the hell have you been?"

"Keeping my head from being blown off. I rather like it where it is."

Taylor couldn't disagree. He looked around to see a motley group, many of which who were at each other's throats just an hour before, but now all looked to him for answers.

"All right, right now we're as deep into this heap of junk as we can be. We need to stick together and get the hell off this thing before it drags us to hell. I need a volunteer who is best suited to guiding us to the surface."

Nobody responded, and he wasn't surprised. It was a lot of responsibility to place on one soul. He looked around for the best person for the job until he finally stopped at Sergeant Lang. He was firmly stuck to Jones' side and eager to be led rather than have to face it all head on.

"Sergeant, you must know the ship better than most. You got point. Lead us out of here."

Lang looked horrified, but Taylor wasn't going to take no for an answer.

"The Nassau has fallen, Sergeant. The only task that remains is your duty to protect her crew. Will you do that?"

He reluctantly nodded in agreement.

"Yes...yes, Sir."

"All right, we take the wounded with us. I'll be up front with the Sergeant here. Jones you bring up the rear, and let's get moving."

A dozen casualties who were still breathing were hauled onto their feet. Taylor knew they would slow the pace substantially, but he could not bring himself to do otherwise. He grabbed a few magazines from one of their own dead at the door and stuffed them into his pouches before slamming one into the rifle. Lang stood next to him and looked down past the line of dead Mechs leading to the bridge. He was in a daze. Parker and Silver moved up to join them.

"Lang, you're leading us, but you stay two paces behind me the whole way, you hear? We can't afford to lose our guide, you got that?"

Taylor could see the relief in Lang's eyes at the realisation he wasn't going to have to go first. He looked back to see the line was now ready to move. Jafar carried one of the wounded on his shoulder with ease while still holding his rifle at the ready. He turned back to Lang.

"You ready?"

A scream echoed from several corridors away, sending a shiver down the Sergeant's back, but he nodded in agreement.

"Okay, let's move out, quick as we can."

He stepped out first.

"You're gonna have to speak up, Sergeant. Guide me."

"Uhhh..."

"Don't think. You know this ship. Walk it like you would any other day of the week."

"Keep going till we reach a flight of stairs directly ahead."

"That's it," he muttered, picking up the pace. Another scream rang out which was much closer now, and they realised they were heading right for the source of it. The stairs were in sight, but as they reached them, a Mech tumbled down and landed at the base. Taylor lifted his rifle to fire at the creature that was flailing to get up. But before he could pull the trigger, a grenade tumbled down the stairs and ignited on the creature. He raised his shield just in time as the blast sent shrapnel flying towards them. He looked up. The metal grid stairs were partly collapsed and now blocked.

"For Christ's sake, can nothing go our way?" he said to himself.

"It's okay. Follow me," replied Lang.

He rushed out to Taylor's left and got up pace down another corridor.

"Back!" he screamed.

Taylor rushed on after him, but he would not slow down. The Colonel looked back. The column could not match their pace with all the wounded. He rushed forward to stop the marine, reaching him at a bend where he had stopped for a moment. Taylor got a firm grasp on his backplate and yanked him back. As he did so, a shot ricocheted off the wall where he had been a second before. Taylor threw the Sergeant behind him as the others got to them. He peaked out around the corner, trying to locate the shooter. The sight of a Mech soldier rapidly advancing towards him at just ten metres away shocked him. Mitch ducked back as more shots landed beside him.

"Right, you son of a bitch," he whispered.

He could hear the steps now. Lang didn't know what to do and couldn't believe Taylor simply waited for the creature to close in on them. Mitch took in a deep breath, and in the last few steps as the Mech got to them, he spun out from the corner and smashed his shield up into the Mech's weapon, driving it high. As the creature's rifle fired into the ceiling, he drove his gun into its stomach and fired on full auto.

The Mech spasmed, its abdomen riddled with bullets. Finally, it went limp. Taylor tossed the body back onto the deck in disgust to reveal the barrel of his rifle that was now drenched in blood. He looked back to Lang who was still speechless.

"You give directions, and I lead. You stay behind me, you hear?"

He nodded and pointed for them to go the way the creature had come from.

"Let's move."

They got ten metres when an explosion rang out not far from their position. Taylor stopped immediately, waiting and listening for anything else. But a moment later, he could hear the sound of running water.

"Oh, shit," he murmured.

His worst fear had come true.

"We're going down, and fast."

Water gushed around a corner up ahead and almost immediately covered their boots. He thought about asking Lang for other options on how to get out, for just a split second, but he knew such indecision could end them as quickly as making the wrong one.

"Keep moving!" he boomed.

He could feel the weight of the water pushing against his feet, and his already exhausted legs were feeling like lead weights trying to drag him down. He struggled on, telling himself he wasn't willing to die down there. As a marine, he knew the situation could occur, and that he might go down with a ship, but he never really thought for one moment it would ever be a possibility.

"Left, left here!"

Taylor followed Lang, took the bend, and found a Mech facing the way they were heading. He didn't even hesitate to fire a burst into its back without breaking stride. The Mech's body splashed into the water as he passed by.

"How many of those fuckers did you have aboard?" Silva asked.

Lang didn't respond. He was clearly feeling more than a little sheepish that he'd been a part of it all. They reached a stairway, and water was already flowing down at quite a rate.

"How do we even know we're still on the surface?"

Taylor didn't reply to Parker's question; he had no good answer. Instead, he leapt onto the stairs and stormed up them. He made it up two flights before looking back to Lang.

"How much further?"

"Not far now. The escape pods are just around the

corner."

Taylor carried on as Lang pointed the way to go. A few bodies swept past them as the water levels were reaching their knees. Debris crashed into his boots and greaves. They took the bend and were met by a line of shuttle doors, each a metre wide.

"No, no!" cried Lang.

Each one of the doors had a thick glass window at the centre and was full with water where the pods had been launched. Every single one was gone.

"Lang, are these the only ones we can use?"

Lang collapsed down onto his knees weeping, but Taylor hauled him back to his feet.

"Concentrate, Sergeant!"

He shook his head. "None that we can reach quickly."

Taylor looked around to the others. They were all waiting for him to come up with a solution.

"I'm not going down with this ship," he stated, "How deep do you reckon we are?"

Jones shrugged. "How the hell can we tell?"

"We haven't been here long. There's still plenty of air and structural integrity from what I've seen."

"Now you're just living on hopes and prays," Rains joined in.

"Yeah, well what else do we have? Ain't no one coming to our rescue. Seal your helmets. We're going for a swim."

Parker shook her head.

"Even if we have got enough air, we open that, and the pressure could kill us instantly."

"And we stay in here, we're dead anyway. I'll take my chances out there. Masks down!"

They quickly responded as he raised his rifle to take aim at one of the pod doors. A second later, he fired a burst at two of the clamps. The door prised open and was launched off its frame by the forces of water gushing in. Taylor turned and looked to Parker; the water had reached his waist. It was their best chance, and they both knew it, but that didn't make it any less terrifying.

They all watched and waited as the water rose up to their masks and then above the doorway. Taylor did not say a word as he activated his boosters and pushed off for the exit. He knew the others would follow without a command. He could not see a thing through the water and only continued to drive upwards, using his arms to swim a little faster. A display light flashed inside his helmet, and he knew exactly what it meant; he was running out of air.

The water was getting lighter and clearer, and suddenly he burst out onto the surface. The warm rays of the sun sitting high in the sky met him. He clicked back the mask on his helmet and breathed in the air with relief; his comrades arose beside him. Parker appeared just a few metres away and swam over to him, wrapping her arms around him.

"We did it!"

"Yeah, we're alive, but for how long?" he said, looking out around them.

Debris lay scattered across the ocean, and they looked up at dozens of alien ships entering the atmosphere overhead.

"Not again, how can this happen again?" pleaded Eli.

"Erdogan, that bastard. We will never know peace while he still draws breath."

CHAPTER TWO

Taylor was looking at the Mappad on his arm, which told him they were a little over a thousand klicks from the Florida coastline.

Believe it when I see it, he thought.

Mitch hadn't been stateside in a long while now, and last time he had, it hardly felt like home. He looked up to see his comrades looked as weary as he did. More than twenty of them were sitting atop one of the many pieces of debris from the Nassau. It looked like one of the double skinned interior walls and at least had good buoyancy.

"Reckon anyone is coming for us, Mitch?" asked Parker.

It was the question on everyone's mind.

"I've tried every channel I can, can't reach a soul."

"Can't be easy to miss a battleship plummeting to Earth," Eddie grinned.

"On any other day you'd be right. But today, who's

29

counting how many ships have entered the atmosphere? It's chaos everywhere."

"Well, you're a beacon of hope."

As Parker said it, they heard a roar of engines in the sky and looked up half expecting to see Mech forces descending upon them. Taylor lifted his hand to shield his eyes from the sun's rays and squinted to make them out. He stood up and gripped his rifle with his other hand, but he quickly recognised they were not of alien construction. One of the ships descended to just two metres above the water, and a lower hull door opened, revealing Captain King in the entrance.

"Looks like you need a ride?"

Taylor couldn't believe their luck, though he knew deep down it wasn't luck at all. He had good people he could depend on.

"Your timing is impeccable."

"Well whatta ya know, takes the Rangers to save leathernecks from the wet stuff. Don't ever think you'll be living this one down."

Taylor smiled in response and could not help but take it in good spirits, after having been left adrift on the ocean. He looked around to at King's other ships hauling crew from the water. He took a running jump and leapt up into the doorway with the Captain.

"What are your orders, Colonel?" he asked.

He looked overhead to see three huge enemy craft

looming over them and heading west for the east coast of the United States. He looked back across the open ocean to the east and thought of the friends they had left there, but he knew what he had to do.

"Too long have we fought on foreign soil; good old US of A needs us, whether she knows it or not. Set a course for Quantico. We're heading home."

"Quantico?" King asked.

"Last I knew it's where General White was. We ain't exactly on best terms, but he's as good as any place to start. Contact them once we're en route to alert them of our arrival."

"Comms are jammed. We've got a few klicks range and that's about all."

"Well that's fucking great. Nice to know some things never change."

As Sergeant Lang came aboard, King looked out at the other crew of the Nassau still lying stranded at sea in life pods and various other pieces of debris.

"What about them? We can't take many more."

Taylor looked out and could see a ship's silhouette in the distance.

"Make a fly past of whatever that vessel is, and alert them to the crewmembers that need recovering."

"And if they don't want to get involved? Can't even see if it's one of ours from here, could just as well be civilian."

"I don't give a shit who it is. There are people in the

water who need help, and they're gonna give it."

Two hours later the coast of America was in sight. Taylor knew he should be glad to see it, but he wasn't. In the distance to the south, he could see enemy vessels over Norfolk and a similar sight over New Jersey to the north.

"What do we do?" asked King.

They were standing in the cockpit with the pilot and co-pilot, astonished by what they were seeing and looking for direction.

"Continue as planned. There'll be whole divisions slugging it out down there. We've done enough for now."

"Enough?" King asked, "Hardly looks like it."

"Today the war became an entirely different animal, one we are all familiar with though. We need to get back to whoever is in command around here, and work out what the hell is going on and what we can do."

As they approached Quantico, a warning light flashed, and the pilot quickly piped up.

"We've just been locked by local air defences."

A transmission came in as they closed in to comms distance.

"Identify yourselves immediately, or you will be fired upon."

The pilot gave his credentials, and the line went silent.

"Hold position and await further communication. Do not enter Quantico air space until advised."

Taylor tapped the pilot's shoulder as he went to respond

and stepped up to take over.

"Negative. This is Colonel Mitch Taylor of the Inter-Allied Regiment. We need immediate permission to land, do you hear me?"

There was silence once again for a moment and then a response.

"Negative, hold position and await instructions."

"We're coming in whether you like it or not. We have hundreds of US troops and allies aboard, and we ARE coming in."

Taylor gestured for the pilot to do as such, but he was frozen solid.

"Take us in," Taylor clarified.

The officer shook his head. "They'll shoot us out of the sky."

"Not a chance, trust me. Now do it."

He did as ordered, but his hands were shaking a little at the prospect of being blasted out of the sky by their own side. They began to surge forward, and the base was in sight now. They could see gun towers tracking their movement and missile silos with doors wide open.

"Sure about this?" King asked him.

"Not really," he whispered, "but we either go forward and risk being shot down, or go back where we'll definitely be fired upon."

"Rock and a hard place, then."

"Alter course immediately, or you will be fired upon!"

Nobody responded, so Taylor had to.

"This is Colonel Mitch Taylor. Get me General White immediately. The General will clear us to land."

"Hold your current position to confirm."

"That's a negative. We're coming in. If you can't confirm we are friendlies, that's your problem. We've just fought through hell to get back here, and I won't wait another minute to get down on the ground. If you want to be responsible for the deaths of hundreds of Americans and our allies, you pull the trigger. Otherwise, stand down and get the General on the line."

The comms went silent as they passed over the air space of Quantico, and they could see a few of the gun towers tracking their position. They were waiting for them to open fire at any moment when finally General White appeared on the screen before them.

"Taylor? That you?"

"Yes, Sir."

"What the hell are you doing, and where the hell have you been? Get your ass on the ground now!"

Taylor smiled. "Just what we've been trying to do, General."

"Well do it quicker."

The transmission ended, and finally a voice came over the comms once again and said sternly, "You are cleared to land at sector 19F."

"And you couldn't have just waited for that?" the pilot

asked Taylor, "We could have had our butts blown out the sky there."

"And we would have been left hanging a few hours if we waited in line for them to go through proper channels."

They were soon on the ground, and as Taylor's boots hit the surface, his name was being called. A Lieutenant strode up and saluted him.

"Sir, General White requests your presence immediately."

"Yeah, thought he might."

Taylor looked around at their surroundings. They were on home soil, but he didn't recognise it. He'd not been to Quantico in as long as he could remember.

"Sir, I must insist on haste, as was made clear to me by the General."

He looked back to King and Jones; both were waiting for his command.

"You can be guaranteed we'll be heading for the eye of the fucking storm before long, so get whatever food, rest, and supplies you can."

"So eloquently put," Jones replied.

The Lieutenant didn't say another word as he drove Taylor to a command and control facility. He was shown through without a single check into a command centre that was packed out with projection displays and several dozen personnel. General White stood at the head of a large table with his command staff surrounding him.

He looked up and shook his head when he saw Taylor approaching.

"Colonel, what the hell happened up there? I don't know whether to arrest you or give you a goddamn medal."

"Then do neither, Sir."

White shook his head once again and took in a deep breath.

"You're a son of a bitch, Mitch, but don't ever forget you are our son of a bitch."

He relaxed a little as he leaned against the table and looked at the 3d relief map projected before them. It showed enemy craft in real time, and he could see air force fighter wings en route to engage.

"Nobody has heard from you since you took off to disable the Earth Defence Grid. The results of which are mostly clear, but I have been authorised to conduct a debriefing for the President. Make it quick," said White.

Taylor looked around, and all eyes were now on him.

"It was a trap. There was no way we could disable all those weapons. All we could do was destroy them. Which we did, and is precisely what Erdogan wanted."

"How do you know that?"

"Because he came to me, as a hologram or whatever. He's mocking us, and he has a right to. He led us exactly where he wanted to, and look where we are now."

"So that's it?"

"That's all that's important."

White nodded. He clearly hadn't expected any better news.

"So it is Erdogan this time?"

"Afraid so. But he's the one, the one that holds it all together. We finish him, and it's over for good."

"I think we have more imminent concerns right now."

Taylor looked shocked.

"We're losing ground fast. We are getting reports of enemy forces throughout the United States and EA nations. It's a mess, Mitch. Honestly, I don't know if we can make it through this one."

Taylor was taken aback and looked around expecting some of the other officers to call him up on his defeatist attitude, but he could see they were no different.

"The invasion isn't even a day through yet, and you are giving up?" he asked them all.

Nobody responded.

"We are fighting and dying out there while you lot cry and cower in your bunker. Well, fuck you, fuck you all."

White was ashamed enough that he did not answer, despite Taylor's ridicule. The room was silent as everyone waited for Taylor to continue and give them some answers.

"We have just one choice here. We fight or we die. I didn't fight all these years to lie down and die now after all that. Can you honestly tell me that everything we did these past few years was for nothing? No, we have beaten these bastards more than once. We've beaten everything they

37

have thrown at us, and now is the final hurdle. Erdogan himself."

"What do we do?" asked one of the other officers at the table.

"What we always do, stand and fight," Taylor quickly retorted.

"If you'd not destroyed our defences, maybe we wouldn't have to be fighting on our own soil," snapped one of the other Generals.

Taylor turned and looked in disgust at the man who he didn't recognise. The General was a good few pounds overweight and looked like a man who'd never seen combat in his life. His face was red and sweaty, which only exaggerated the shine on his baldhead. He was all Taylor despised in armchair generals.

"Yeah, and maybe if I'd not gone up there, Washington would be a wasteland right about now, along with a dozen or more cities around the World. I did what had to be done. I'm not saying it was the perfect solution, but it was the best of a bad bunch."

"You have single-handedly opened up the doors for this invasion which could be the end of us all!"

"Well you pompous, arrogant, naive asshole!" Taylor yelled.

"Enough!" White boomed.

He looked to the General. His face was fuming.

"General Gomez, the last thing we need right now is to

be arguing over what might have been. And you, Colonel, you may be a valuable asset, but that does not make you above the chain of command or beyond common courtesy. What is quite clear is that we need to go forward, and that will not happen while we stand here having a pissing contest."

They all now looked to White for answers.

"As you are all well aware, the enemy comms jamming caused us some serious issues. We still have direct feeds operational to DC and most of the East Coast bases. National Guard in New York is taking an absolute beating, and the marines in Norfolk are having it just as bad. We do not expect either location to hold beyond the day."

It was a shock to Taylor. He'd spent so long fighting on foreign soil that the prospect of American cities being fought over was utterly alien to him. He knew such battles had been fought before, but he had never been in such proximity that it felt so real.

The General opened his mouth to speak, but before he got another word out, a warning light flashed, and a siren sounded throughout the room. They all looked around for answers, but the live update information on the map before them displayed the danger. More than a dozen enemy vessels were approaching, and the base defences that had come so close to firing upon Taylor and his unit were already lit up. Missile trails and tracers lit up the map as the fight played out like a video game.

"Sir, troops and armoured vehicles are descending from incoming targets," stated one of the officers at a console beside the table.

"In what number?" White asked.

"Hard to tell, Sir, but we have detected well over three hundred Mechs to the east perimeter and more closing in from the south."

"I want everyone on base able to walk armed and at their stations immediately!"

He looked back to Taylor.

"How many men have you got with you?"

"A few hundred."

"Will they fight?"

"Always."

"Then we need you. Head to the southern perimeter and do what you do best."

"Yes, Sir," Taylor replied with a smile.

The situation sucked and Mitch was well aware of it. But heading out to fight Mech warriors was a relief after being confined to petty arguments in the stuffy Command and Control Centre. He pulled on his helmet and strode out of the building to find the Lieutenant who had driven him there still waiting beside his vehicle.

"You got a weapon?"

"I can draw one, Sir."

"Then do it now. I'm taking your ride."

Taylor threw his rifle in through the open-sided light

40

vehicle and climbed in before the Lieutenant could argue. Mitch stamped on the gas, and the jeep raced forward, but he couldn't hear the almost silent engine over the screams of marines nearby and explosions igniting around the complex. He remembered the way back to where he had landed, and only hoped to find his comrades still in the vicinity. Pulses soared through the sky and smashed into buildings around him. He could see one coming right for him almost in slow motion. He quickly snapped the steering to avoid it.

The lightweight unarmoured vehicle went up and on its side wheels and to the apex of tipping. Taylor leaned out and used his bodyweight to keep it from rolling over. The vehicle crashed back down onto the ground, and he held onto the steering for dear life as the rear end fishtailed a little before coming back into line. The little jeep wasn't built for this. It was a light, fast utility, and the last thing he wanted to be in when the firing started.

Another pulse as large as his vehicle smashed into the ground in front of him, creating a half-metre deep crater. His jeep dropped down into it and then ramped up and out the other side, launching the wheels off the ground. As he landed, he could see airborne Mechs descending around him. He picked up his rifle with one hand, rested the barrel over the front cowl, and fired on full auto at one that landed next to him. Three shots penetrated its armour before he rammed the creature.

The thick rail design construction caused the jeep to initially knock the dead Mech to the ground and then ramp over it, lifting two side wheels off the ground once again. He took a bend up ahead and slid around the corner where he found a line of troops dug in at a five-metre high wall with towers every twenty metres. Turreted heavy weapons on the towers were firing as quickly as their autoloaders would allow them. He brought the jeep to a halt and immediately heard his name being called. "Taylor!"

He turned. Parker was crouching in the doorway of a building to his right. He jumped out of the jeep and had gotten only three metres from it when a pulse struck it dead on. The explosion launched him into the air, tossing him into the building where Parker was positioned. He landed hard but quickly huddled up beside her for protection. He looked back at his vehicle, and nothing more than a few twisted pieces of roll bar and a single wheel were still recognisable.

"You okay?" screamed Eli, grabbing him and looking over his body for injuries.

"Yeah, yeah, I'm fine," he said, trying to regain his senses.

"Guess we came to the wrong place!" she yelled.

"I figure we're exactly where we need to be," he replied dryly.

She couldn't help but smile at his optimism.

"Where is everyone?"

"Scattered. King is up on that wall helping with the defences. Jones is keeping an eye on the Nassau crew and marines we brought back. Last I saw, Silva was with him. Most of my platoon is here with me."

"Which way is Jones?"

She pointed, and he rushed on without another word. He took a corner and found Jones standing guard over the German marines and sailors as if they were POWs. They had their backs to the wall, blocking their line of sight from the southern wall and providing some protection.

"Guess we're bolstering the defences?" he asked Jones.

"You got it."

He looked over at the German weapons stacked at a far wall. Taylor immediately strode up to Sergeant Lang.

"You've seen what we're up against," he looked around and spoke up to address them all, "I'll be frank. We took some losses up there against UEN forces. Losses we could not afford. But you lot stood with us when we needed it most. The Inter-Allied Regiment is not an EA Regiment, not a UEN Regiment, nor an American Regiment. We stand for the defence of Earth, no matter which nation you come from. I am gonna make you all a onetime offer. Right now you are prisoners of war. You may continue as such and hope we win this war while you sit it out in a cell. Or you can join us. Take up your weapons and join the Regiment. What do you say?"

"You would have us?" Lang asked in surprise.

43

"You all showed you could handle yourselves up there. I need fighters. You want to live. I think it's a more than fair deal. The sailors among you will be reassigned to whatever craft of ships when we get them. But I expect every one of the personnel under my command to take up a rifle and use it. So what'll it be?"

Lang looked around to his comrades for their approval but could already see they were of one mind. He turned back to Taylor and simply replied rather succinctly, "Yes."

"Then welcome to the war. You will all retain your rank, and for now, Sergeant, you will command your comrades as a platoon under my Company."

"Thank you," he replied, following it with a salute.

"Grab you weapons, and get your asses in this fight!"

They rushed for the horde of weapons and gear as Jones stepped up beside Taylor.

"Sure this is a good idea?"

"We can't take prisoners, and we need all the help we can get. We won the last wars because humanity stood together. If we can't do it this time, what hope is there?"

Jones wanted to disagree, but as he did so, an explosion erupted above. Taylor looked up; a Mech ship was hurtling out of control towards them.

"Cover!"

He leapt down against the wall of the nearest building. The craft plunged into the upper floors, sending bricks and masonry falling down all around them. Mitch felt several bricks smash into his helmet and jolt his neck. He got up; the dust was settling, and the rest of them were getting to their feet. He looked around for the remnants of the craft, and there was a hole in a two-storey complex opposite where it had penetrated right through. He raised his rifle with suspicion.

A moment later his suspicions were confirmed. Three Mechs leapt through the breach and landed amongst them. Taylor's finger squeezed the trigger of his rifle as the first creature landed, and a line of automatic fire strafed mid section. The weapon the Mech carried was cut in two, but the shots didn't seem to penetrate its armour.

The weight of fire cut down one of the other creatures, but the unarmed one now rushed at him like a raging bull. He kept firing but only got a few shots off. It barged him with all its weight and sent him hurtling back through the wall he had been using for cover just a few moments before. Taylor's shield was ripped from his arm as he burst through the wall and landed firmly on his back.

He was staggering to get to his feet when the wall gave way further, and the creature stormed through to continue its assault against him. His hands were empty, so he reached quickly for his Assegai. As it bore down on him, it was riddled in the back from gunfire and fell hard before it was able to reach his position. He took a deep breath and sighed in relief, and then looked down at the creature that had proven so difficult to kill. Its armour appeared a little thicker and a different construction to what he had seen so many times before.

Jafar stepped through into the room and reclaimed his weapons. He tossed the dead creature over so he could look at it from the front. Taylor could hear the gunfire nearby had come to an end, but he was more than a little curious and concerned about the fallen enemy.

"I opened up on this one, and it did fuck all, what's the deal?" he demanded of Jafar.

His alien friend looked as surprised as he did and bent down to take a closer look.

"What's the deal?" Taylor asked impatiently.

"I have not seen this before."

"Not seen it? Well that's a big fucking help. A burst in the torso from a Reitech rifle did nothing; we need to know something, as this is gonna be a big ass problem."

Jafar raised his rifle and fired a point blank shot into the creature's sternum, and then knelt down to look at the impact. His fingers passed over the surface.

"The bullet has impacted and stopped."

"These are high AP rounds, how can that be? Must be some new tech."

"Is it such a surprise that the enemy would improve over time its weapons and equipment, just as we have?"

Taylor shrugged his shoulders. It made sense, but he still didn't like hearing it.

"How about the other Mechs out there? Same?"

"It took many shots to take them down."

"Casualties?"

"A few."

Taylor stepped back out through the hole he had been thrown to hear the sound of war was now all around. Explosions and volleys of gunfire were especially frequent towards the south wall, and pulses continued to smash their positions from the enemy ships above, providing brutal ground support. One of the German sailors lay dead, and a marine was wounded, as well as one of their own being patched up. They looked to him for something.

"They've up armoured, up gunned, and upped their game. If we want to win this war, we're gonna have to do the same, just as we always have. But right now, we have to survive."

As he said it, a pulse struck the ground only a metre from him, and he looked up at more Mechs descending from the sky.

"Incoming!" he yelled.

They all scattered for cover, and Taylor leapt partially into the hole he had been thrown in before. He took aim and fired several shots into one of the Mechs, killing it instantly. But as he took aim at his next target, he noticed the new armour pattern once again. He fired several shots, but none seemed to penetrate.

"Goddamn it!" he muttered to himself.

As the creature landed, he took aim at its head, firing a

three-shot burst, but two were deflected from the sloped and pointed faceplate while the third seemed to embed but not go through. He let his rifle drop to his side, drew out his Assegai, and rushed at the alien; his shield held forward and tilted back to try and deflect energy. He felt a pulse strike it and saw the light particles burst past either side of his shield. A second later he barrelled into the Mech soldier, and it felt good to be the one dealing out some punishment.

The impact was enough to knock the Mech back a few paces, but it quickly got its footing and ground to a halt. Taylor could feel the mass of the creature because he would have been able to throw a normal Mech over with such a ferocious charge. He hooked a thrust around the edge of his Assegai and felt it meet the creature's armour, though he could not see where.

Without warning, a thunderous strike smashed into his shield. Taylor felt it break in the centre, and he heard a crunch and felt his left arm go numb; the numbness and tingling sensation was immediately followed by pain surging up through his arm, and he felt it droop. His arm was broken, for sure, but he could not pause to check it. He looked back, and the Mech was swinging its weapon like a huge club at his head. He ducked under the strike and drove his Assegai up into its torso, stabbing again and again until the Mech began to slump.

The creature was collapsing down towards him, and he

spun around just in time to avoid being crushed beneath its corpse. He immediately cupped his injured arm with the other and retreated back against a wall. He saw Jafar snap one of the Mech's arms, the armour plating tearing apart, and he drove an Assegai through the open plate.

The air was thick with the smell of sweat, blood, and scorched flesh. It was what Taylor hated worst about war, the acrid smell and taste of it. Parker rushed to his side, and he could see the concern in her face.

"You all right?"

He nodded.

"No really, Mitch, don't bullshit me!"

"I'm fine. Left arm is fucked, but I'm fine."

She looked down at the joint of his Reitech suit. It was snapped at the elbow and barely held together. It was clear to both of them it had been all that had stopped his arm being snapped in two. She ran her hand over his arm to feel for the injury and stopped as he winced.

Gunfire raged all around, and Mitch was glad to see his people were fighting as hard as ever. His attention was drawn to Sergeant Lang who was in the thick of the action and proving himself a worthy member of the unit.

"We gotta get you out of here, Mitch," said Parker.

He grunted in disapproval, still keeping a firm grip on his Assegai and with plenty of fight left in him.

"You're no good to us like this. Come on, follow me," she stated, looking around for an opening to get him out.

"Medic!" she screamed.

CHAPTER THREE

The roof shook every few moments, and Taylor's hand crept nearer to the rifle lying on the table beside his bed.

"Leave it!" Parker shouted.

He leant back and sat upright on the bed he had been waiting on.

"My arm's fucked, not my body," he snapped back.

A pulse hit the roof and burst through, striking two of the beds occupied by wounded soldiers. Taylor leapt for cover as it landed, and fragments of the pulse burst across the room. They punched through the divider the other side of him, and he reached for his helmet with his good arm.

"I need two seconds with a doc, and I'll be back in action. Find me one!" he ordered.

Parker nodded in agreement and rushed off in search of one. They both knew he needed to be in the fight, and a few seconds later she reappeared, hauling a doctor by the collar of his coat while he protested.

"Please, there are people who need my help," he whimpered.

She shoved him towards Taylor and let go.

"Get the Colonel back in this fight, or these patients may not live long enough for any of your work to matter."

The doctor looked back and began to hesitate but was interrupted by Taylor's rather unsubtle cough to get his attention. The man looked around to see the Colonel sitting before him; the expression on Mitch's face instantly silenced him.

"All right, what do you need?"

"Fix my arm, Doc."

He looked at it for a minute and put pressure down in different areas. It wasn't a case of finding where his arm was wounded, but which part was the most damaged. Another explosion hit the roof of the building and sent a cloud of dust into the air.

"Haven't got all day, Doc. Get it done."

"I can fix it now, but it will be weak for several days at least, maybe a few weeks."

Taylor nodded in agreement.

The doctor pulled out a syringe and injected into his arm.

"We need to get all this off. I need the arm bare."

Taylor tried to unclip his body armour, but the pain

was too much, and he gritted his teeth as he felt the shock through his body.

"Here, I'll get it," said Parker.

He didn't like being helpless, but he had no choice. She stripped the Reitech armour and suit from his upper body and pulled his shirt off. The doctor stopped in surprise at his body. It looked as if it was cut from steel. Years of training and war had shaped him into what looked like a professional ring fighter, but his skin was covered in bruising and old scars. The doctor could not help but stare.

"I ain't pretty, but I ain't a model either," Taylor stated.

Parker smiled.

"Lie down please," replied the doctor, snapping out of his daze, "I'll need to get my equipment."'

He did as asked by the doctor. Parker loomed over him and took his good hand in his.

"How do you do it?" she whispered.

"Do what?"

"Keep surviving?"

He had no answer for her. The doctor rushed back into the room, clearly trying to get it over with as quickly as possible so he could move on to other patients. He carried a device for resetting and repairing limbs and joints that Taylor had seen more than a few times, though he was still none the wiser as to how the wondrous machine worked. It was slipped over his arm and clamped in place at either end. It made him wince a little; the doctor was far from gentle at his rushed pace.

A screen lit up on the device showing an x-ray of his arm, and within a minute the doctor had programmed it ready. Lights lit up in the machine as it began to operate, and the man finally looked up to Taylor.

"In about five minutes time it will power down, and you will be finished here. Now please, Colonel, I must leave you and attend to others."

"All right, Doc, and thanks."

He scurried off. Taylor looked down at the machine and felt several needle like implements pierce his skin. A few seconds later he lost feeling in the arm, which at least deadened the pain, but it also dulled the rest of his senses and made him a little drowsy. He did his best to hide it from Parker, but she noticed. She opened her mouth to speak, but Taylor interrupted.

"Don't. I know what you're going to say, but there's no time for it."

She looked puzzled.

"I was just gonna say, we made it again."

Taylor smiled, but they heard another few eruptions outside the building that shook the ceiling.

"We aren't out of the fire quite yet."

Gunfire erupted a few metres outside the room, and Eli turned quickly, raising her rifle.

"Go to it!" Taylor said quietly.

She looked back and hesitated, but the determined look he responded with made her turn and do as ordered. Parker rushed through one of the hospital corridors that were littered with both wounded and dead. A few held rifles where they lay, but no one other than herself looked ready for a real fight.

"Shit," she muttered.

She edged forward more cautiously and felt her hands instinctively grip tighter around her rifle. Too tightly in fact, which made her swear at herself for not keeping calm and remembering her training. A wall collapsed in a few metres ahead. A soldier flew through it and hit the wall the other side of the corridor. She moved to go to his aid but stopped as more of the wall was smashed through, and a Mech rushed into view.

Before the creature could turn and face her head on, Parker's rifle was firing. She got off five shots as it snapped around, but the damage she had inflicted made it fire wildly. Pulses ripped through the corridor amongst the wounded. Parker shifted to the opposite wall and kept up the fire. Ten shots had penetrated the creature's armour by the time she got within striking distance, and it dropped to its knees so that its head was in line with hers.

Eli did not hesitate or take any chances. Her rifle fired again, and a burst of shots ripped into the faceplate of the Mech; it slumped dead to the floor. She looked over to the soldier who had been thrown into the corridor and knelt down to feel his pulse, but he was gone. She shook her head and looked back down the corridor. Only two of the troops lining the sides were still alive, and they looked terrified.

Parker wanted to go back to them but knew she had a responsibility to go. She stepped over the body of her victim and continued on as the lights began flickering above. Gunfire still raged in the distance, but she could hear nothing of an enemy presence nearby, so much so it made her suspicious.

She took a bend into another ward and found dozens of wounded being attended to. She carried on through, heading for the main entrance of the facility. As she grew nearer, she found a wounded Ranger from their unit. He was sitting up against a doorway, with his rifle at the ready but clearly unable to stand. She could see corporal stripes on his uniform and recognised him as one of their own but not his name. He turned and acknowledged her as she approached.

"You all right?" she asked sympathetically, kneeling down at the far side of the door.

"Still breathing," he replied.

She looked closer to make out his name, 'Vidal, anyone else here with you?"

He shook his head and pointed over to the bodies of two marines who had clearly fallen very recently. She shook her head.

This place is turning into a fucking morgue!

"You just hold on, Corporal. We'll get you out of here."

"I ain't going anywhere anytime soon," he replied, with a small smile that could not hide the pain he was feeling.

Parker got to her feet and had to keep telling herself to go forward and towards the light of the open doors ahead. A trail of bodies, both alien and human, trailed all the way to the entrance and outside. As she reached the end of the corridor, she could hear a hive of activity outside and leapt to the sidewall, ready to fire at whatever came through.

Her heart almost stopped, and the lack of oxygen as she held her breath made her feel a little dizzy. A shadow appeared at the door, and a body followed it soon after. She lifted her rifle to fire, realising just as she was about to pull the trigger that it was Jones. She nearly fell over, quickly pulled her rifle back, and took a deep breath.

"Parker, you okay?" Jones asked, seemingly not bothered at all by the gun in his face. He looked more concerned for her safety than his own.

"Where is Taylor?" he asked more sternly.

She pointed to where she had come from.

"Getting fixed up."

"Lead the way."

She did as ordered but could not go on without asking questions.

"How is it out there?"

"Rough, but we're holding fast."

"So what's the plan?"

He shook his head. "Your guess is as good as mine. I don't even know who is in charge here."

They reached the wounded ranger, who was still waiting with his rifle at the ready. Jones did not even break stride but clearly recognised the man.

"You keep doing what you're doing, Corporal," he said to Vidal as he passed.

"Yes, Sir," he replied confidently.

It seemed cold and uncompassionate at first, but Parker could see the rise in Vidal's eyes, being addressed as a soldier and not a casualty. It impressed her. Her natural reaction was to ask after his wellbeing, when he clearly was able and willing to fight. They carried on past the body of the Mech she had killed and those of many more humans who had been killed by the aerial bombardments. Eli led them to Taylor's room, but as they went into it, she stopped and gasped. The bed was empty, and only the device Mitch that had been connected to his arm remained.

"Where is the Colonel?" Jones asked.

She was at a loss for words.

"Where the hell is he?"

She turned; realising Jones wasn't addressing her but merely venting his frustration.

"Captain Jones!"

They turned and rushed towards the sound of the call

58

to a blown out window around the corner. They were two floors up, and rubble was dropping past their window from where the roof was being bombarded. Troops were still battling Mechs in the divide between them and the tall perimeter fence. It took a few seconds for either of them to spot Taylor until the messenger pointed him out. Mitch was climbing a gun tower where they could see the two crewmembers atop it lying dead, and a large hole in the three-metre wide shield of the weapon system.

"What the hell are you doing, Mitch?" Jones hollered.

They looked up to see more enemy ships roaring overhead and continuing to bombard the base, with little fire opposing them.

"He's gonna get himself killed!" screamed Parker.

Without another word, she leapt out of the window and descended as quickly as she safely could to the ground below. As she came to a stop, she saw Mitch climbing into the firing seat of the gun emplacement. She could see the remotely controlled towers were knocked out and pouring with smoke. Taylor's position was the only anti-aircraft emplacement still operational in their vicinity.

"Mitch!" she called out to him.

She tapped her communicator, calling for him once again, but there was no response. She began to run towards the tower. She could see the turret rotate and begin to target an enemy craft. It was large, spanning more than thirty metres in length and looked like a gunship transport of some kind.

The twin-barrelled guns Taylor controlled opened fire, and a missile launched a few seconds later. The enemy ship was first raked with fire, and she could see more than a dozen Mechs bailing out the side. Finally, the missile struck, and an explosion ripped through the hull. A smoke trail span out from the ship as it began to lose control and bank towards the tower. Parker watched in horror. She could already see it was heading for Taylor.

"Mitch!"

There was no chance he could hear her, but it was all she could do, and she felt helpless to save the one she loved more than any other in the world. Taylor kept his finger on the trigger, and gunfire continued to rip through the burning craft, but he could see there was nothing he could do to stop it. The wreck was soaring towards his position. He leapt out from the seat and ran to the edge of the tower with all the strength and speed he could muster.

Taylor leapt from the edge and could feel the heat of the craft as it impacted and ignited on striking the tower. The blast propelled him further forward than he had expected, and he felt a heavy impact in the back plate of his armour. He was thrown onto the rooftop of a parked truck and slid off to the ground the other side. He tumbled several times, coming to a halt on his side.

Parker had seen the whole thing and still stood in shock. She had not even sheltered herself from the blast, and debris lay everywhere around her. She stepped forward to go where she had seen Mitch land, but two Mechs landed before her. There was no fear now left in her, for the only thing she cared about was Mitch. She rushed at the two Mechs, knowing it was overly ambitious. Her finger had already found the trigger as she took her first step and fired on the move.

As she rushed at the first creature, she caught a glimmer of movement out of the corner of her eye and saw Jafar descend on the other Mech like a pile driver and smash it down to the ground. He smashed the stock of his rifle through the faceplate, and blue blood burst out across the ground. By the time she had reached the other creature, she had emptied what was left in her magazine, and it was dead on its feet, but that did not stop her. She rushed into the Mech and knocked it stone cold dead into the blood soaked asphalt.

The impact with the creature knocked her a little off balance and spun her around, but she got her footing and kept running on towards Taylor. "Mitch!" Gunfire sounded around her, but she paid it no attention. She reached the truck he had landed on and could see a sizeable dent in the roof, but she kept going. She finally saw him, but he wasn't moving. He lay on his side, almost in a recovery position.

"Mitch! Mitch! No!"

She knelt down and shook him.

"Easy!" he suddenly croaked.

She took a sigh in relief and dropped her head down onto him, finding her helmet crashing into his armour. It was as close as she would get to affection in the heat of battle. She looked up and into his eyes.

"Are you okay? Can you move?"

He groaned.

"I don't know," he whispered quietly.

She looked terrified.

"Move, goddamn it!"

Jones arrived at the scene and rushed up beside them.

"You're still alive then, you silly bastard?"

Taylor nodded with a smile.

"Oh, come on, get up," Jones continued.

He reached up and grabbed Jones' armour around the neck, hauling himself up onto his feet. Taylor felt several bones in his body creek as he was forced to stand on his own feet and staggered a little. Only Jones' hold stopped him from toppling over.

"See, still standing," said Jones.

He let go, and Taylor's legs wobbled a little until he just about managed to stabilise himself. He could instantly see the worry in Parker's eyes.

"I'm fine, just a little shook up."

In fact, although his arm had been fixed, it still hurt like hell, but it was now just one in a long list of pains he could feel.

"What's the deal?" he asked, as if expecting Jones and

Parker to have more information than him.

They all looked up; the enemy vessels in the air had been thinned out. Although fighting was still going on throughout the base, it seemed they were now in control. Taylor looked around to see more of his unit now surrounding him. They were all looking to him for answers, but he knew he had no good ones.

"We can't stay here. We may have held this attack off, but they'll be back. We need to find General White and work out what the hell is going on."

"I can see what's going on. We're getting a lashing."

Taylor couldn't disagree with Jones but tried to regain his composure.

"Parker, your platoon is with me. Jones, dig in here, and hold until I can work out what's going on."

Jones immediately leapt into action and began yelling his orders. Taylor strode forward. He was more than a little unstable on his feet, but he did everything he could to hide it and kept putting one foot in front of the other, hoping the forward motion would keep him going.

The base was in chaos. Troops were still attempting to sweep and clear all remaining Mechs. Wounded lay scattered amongst the dead, and vehicles lay strewn about in various conditions. Some of the wreckage was barely indistinguishable between human and alien creation; it was so twisted and wrecked. A fallen Mech in front of them began moving just a little, but a second later was met by a burst from Parker's rifle, which finished it for good.

"Nice," Taylor muttered.

A burst of gunfire rang out from a Mech pulse weapon. One of the heavily armed creatures was blazing away in the open while brushing off multiple shots from troops using cover all around to try and take it down. Taylor stopped for a moment with the intent to go and help, but before he could take another step, an armoured transport vehicle raced into view and struck the creature head on. The Mech was smashed down and run under the wheels of the heavy vehicle. Within seconds, a dozen troops stood over its body, emptying their magazines to finish it off.

"That's how to do it."

Taylor grunted. "Yeah, Parker, but we gotta find a few other ways of taking 'em down."

They carried on to where Taylor had last seen the Generals but found half of the building he had left was now flattened. Bodies were still being pulled from the ruins by surrounding personnel. He could see a few officers sitting about the rubble in shock.

"This doesn't look good," whispered Parker.

Taylor carried on towards them and was pleased to see one was General White. His uniform was cut at the arm, and blood was seeping out over the sleeve. He was covered in a thick coating of dust. He was simply peering out into the distance as if oblivious to all that was going on around him.

"General, General White!" Taylor said, stepping up in front of him.

White slowly turned and looked at Mitch, but his eyes were wide open, his expression a combination of terror and surprise.

"You okay, Sir?"

No response came for a few moments until White finally coughed and cleared his throat. He was starting to come back to reality.

"What are your orders, Sir?"

He seemed confused and shook his head. Taylor leaned in closer.

"We need leadership right now, and that has to come from you. There are plenty around here who have had it a lot worse than you."

White nodded in agreement, and his eyes seem to show he was recovering his composure.

"Taylor? What are you still even doing here? You ain't a marine no more."

"I'm whatever I need to be, and I will always be a marine," he replied, reaching down to haul the General to his feet.

"So you'll stand with us?" asked White.

"Always."

He took in a deep breath, sighing as he regained his composure, and stood up a little taller and a little prouder.

"Much of my staff were killed here, and it looks like

the personnel on base suffered about as bad."

"How's the rest of the coast doing? New York? Philly?"

"Both have fallen. Survivors of New York have gone inland. National Guard and Army regulars out of Philly are falling back on Baltimore. Last orders received were to support them there."

"Is that still the case?"

"It's as good a plan as any. At least we can amass some firepower in one place. Corps Reserves out of Harrisburg are on the way also, and anyone else who can make it."

"And if we circle the wagons, and they drop a tactical nuke or whatever shit they got like it, on our heads?" Taylor asked.

"I'd rather die fighting beside our own than picked off one-by-one."

"Fair enough, can't argue with that."

Taylor couldn't help but feel their situation was more desperate than it had ever been. They were better prepared and equipped, and yet were falling as quickly as the first invasion of Earth. The General looked around for any of his staff and reached out to the first one he recognised who was staggering past with her arm in a sling.

"I want every transport, every armoured vehicle, and every fighting man and woman loaded up and en route to Baltimore in the next thirty minutes."

The woman looked confused. She was a Lieutenant and clearly one of General White's personal staff.

"You heard the General," Taylor added.

"Aye, aye, Sir," she suddenly responded.

"What do you want of us?" Taylor asked White.

"Force recon, right? I want you to blaze a path to Baltimore for us. Think you can do that?"

"Hell, yes."

* * *

Taylor stood before the craft that had landed them on the base. One was almost cut in two by a crashed fighter, and the others being worked on by their crews, who were desperately trying to get them operational. He caught a glimpse of Rains atop the nearest one, and working on part of one of the turbines.

"This ain't even your bird!" Taylor shouted to him.

"Yeah, well, ain't got one, so it's as close as I can get!"

"Think you'll be airworthy in the next thirty minutes?"

He stopped what he was doing and looked at Taylor as if to ask, 'are you serious?' Taylor simply nodded in return.

"Do what I can!" he yelled back and went back at it.

Taylor was looking over the craft a little closer, and the weapon systems fitted which were few and far between.

"These craft are modular, right? Intended for a range of tasks and quick modification for an intended purpose?"

"Yes," replied King, standing beside him, "What have you got in mind?"

"I want every gun you can possibly find fitted on these birds."

"It's mostly open bay weapon platforms. We do that, and we're limited to low altitude work, and we definitely ain't getting out of the atmosphere."

"That's the last of our concerns right now, Captain. Every weapon system you can muster. "

King nodded in agreement and rushed off to carry out the orders. Within a minute, ground crews were stripping panels from the hulls and wheeling out weapons from a storage facility next to them. He turned around to Jones and Parker.

"Gather up any of our wounded who can still fight. We're taking them with us."

"That a good idea?"

He looked around at the destruction around them and bodies still being carried away.

"They'll be safer with us than anywhere else, Jones, and we need them as much as they need us."

He could see crews lifting heavy Reitech weapons onto the ships. It was as simple as removing metre-square panels in the hull and clamping the weapons in their place for human operation. It was primitive, but it would get them what he wanted.

"When we're up the air next time, I want to rain hell on whoever and whatever we encounter," he stated.

Twenty-five minutes later, the ships were ready to go.

Four vessels were all they had, but each was equipped with six fixed guns on either side of the hull, as well as their nose-mounted cannons and missile launchers.

"Flying Fortresses," said Taylor.

"What?" Parker asked.

"No, he's right," added Rains, "The old B17s, fortresses in the sky."

"I got no idea what you're talking about," she replied.

Taylor only smiled in response as King strode up to them.

"We're ready to roll," he stated.

"Then what are you waiting for? Load up."

He turned to Jones and indicated for him to follow the same order, which he quickly did. Taylor turned and watched the orders issued across comms channels and their personnel leaping into action.

"You know this lot need rest, and so do you," Parker whispered in his ear.

It was true. His arm was still sore from the elbow to shoulder.

"We'll rest when we have time to," he replied softly. He then headed for the nearest craft, which the pilot had rather hurriedly hand painted the name 'Maya'. As he got aboard, he turned back to Jones.

"What's our head count?"

"Two hundred and sixty three, if you count the Germans you invited along for the ride. Twenty of those are wounded but still combat effective. All other casualties have been transferred to medical transports heading west."

He nodded in response. He prayed those casualties made it out alive, but he knew none of them were safe, no matter where they went. Taylor opened a direct channel to General White who had clearly been anticipating his contact.

"We're good to go, Sir."

"Glad to hear it, Colonel. We've got reports of multiple incoming vessels to the east. We need to be in Baltimore pronto!"

"We're lifting off presently. Good luck to you, Sir."

"And you, Colonel."

He stepped up to the pilot's cockpit so he could see everything unfold with his own eyes.

"Take us out."

The engines were already roaring, and they were off the ground almost instantly.

"You know where we're going. Stay low, too many larger vessels prowling the skies. Do not stop or slow down for anything, you hear me?"

"Yes, Sir."

He turned back to the transport bay that was crammed with more troops and ammunition than was ideal. They could barely move over one another.

"Man the guns. Be ready to defend yourselves at all times!"

Parker was the first one to take up position at one of the hull-mounted weapons, and others soon followed suit.

"Why Baltimore?"

Taylor looked down to see Sergeant Lang sitting beside him.

"Baltimore was like a fortress, a bastion in the first war. Layer after layer of bunkers, trenches, and gun emplacements. Like nothing we've ever seen in our lifetimes."

"And it held?"

Taylor took in a breath and shook his head.

"They held a hell off a long time, more than anywhere else on the frontline. Baltimore is a symbol of resistance to Americans, and since the war, it's never really been rebuilt. If we're gonna batten down the hatches and try and make a stand, it's the place to do it."

It was a look of loss and defeat that overcame Lang's face at his words. Even as Taylor was saying them, he knew their situation was dire. They had been in the air for a few minutes, and Taylor was starting to believe they might make it there without incident. It was a moment of hope that would soon be trampled upon.

"Incoming!"

It was the word he had been waiting for and praying would not come. It came from one of the gunners at the starboard side, and Taylor pushed his way through to get a view for himself. As he reached the fixed weapon, the

71

man at it was taking aim. Three ships were incoming that appeared about the size of their own. They were almost in range when dozens of objects started to launch out from the bows of the vessels. Taylor lifted his rifle to use the scope for a better look and instantly recognised the drones as just like those they had been attacked by in France.

"Web rounds!"

He dropped the magazine of his rifle and pulled out the single web round mag with the yellow identification band around its base. As he slammed it in, the gunners on his side opened fire on full auto. Fire was quickly returned, and he could hear impacts peppering the hull like hail on a windshield. As Taylor chambered a round, something impacted on the hull beside the gunner in front of him, and an explosion flashed before them. The gunner was thrown back against him, but Taylor managed to keep the two of them on their feet.

He saw the gun was missing from its mount and had been torn off the ship. The open cabin around it was scorched, and they both realised they were mere centimetres from the deadly missile.

"Too close!" Taylor shouted.

He rushed to the window and quickly raised his rifle. Drones were soaring towards them for another pass. The guns along the hull were still firing, and he saw one of the drones blasted out of the sky. But for all of their ammo expenditure, they were achieving little. He raised his rifle and took aim at two of the drones that were flying close to each other.

Gunfire rushed at their vessel, but Taylor calmed his breathing and squeezed the trigger. The shot rushed from his rifle and expanded out. The web instantly encompassed one of the drones and knocked the other off course. The trapped drone dropped from the sky like a brick.

"It works," he whispered, "Take 'em down!"

Others rushed to the gunports and opened fire with volleys of the web rounds that saw the drones being swatted like flies from fifty metres away. The fixed guns turned their fire to the drone carriers and bombarded them with prolonged bursts. Taylor sighed in relief as the rest of them cheered at their victory. He looked around; Lang and the other Germans were genuinely impressed. He didn't have the heart to tell the Sergeant that the drones were little more than a scouting party.

"Baltimore, here we come!" Parker shouted.

CHAPTER FOUR

Taylor was the first to step down the ramp onto the surface and stopped to look out at the ten-metre high walls either side of them, thinking of how they had seen layers just like it from the air.

"Looks like Minas Tirith," said Lang.

"What?" Silva asked.

"Layer after layer of thick walls housing a city. Tolkien?"

Silva shook his head and that brought a smile to Jones' face.

"We'll bring some culture to your world yet," he added.

Silva was still oblivious to what they were talking about and shrugged it off.

A dozen friendly vessels passed overhead, coming in to land throughout the city, and many more could be seen on the ground. Troops and vehicles were busy at work all around them.

"Will it be enough?"

"Probably not, Jones," replied Taylor.

Jones could not help but laugh at his scepticism, to avoid crying instead. Taylor was looking around for some semblance of authority. Army and Marine personnel were intermingled, and he could make out the uniforms of cops and Coast Guard. National Guard and Marine reservists were there too.

"One big happy family," said Silva.

A stripped down utility mule jeep parted some of the troops and stopped by them. It had just a single seat for the driver; the rest being a flat topped carrying deck.

"Colonel Taylor?" asked the driver.

"Yeah," he replied casually.

"Sir, General Heath requests your presence immediately, and that of Captain Jones if he is with you."

"And he couldn't have called this in?"

"Comms are haywire, Sir. We've got interference coming in all over the place, and we have no idea who is listening in. Fixed line communications have been established every one hundred metres on all the walls for when they are needed."

"Going old school."

"Yes, Sir."

"King, you know what to do. We'll be back shortly." Taylor climbed onto the flat-topped vehicle with Jones.

"Sorry about the ride, Sir, but we're a little hard pressed

right now."

The driver raced off, causing troops nearby to jump out of the way. Taylor and Jones hung on rather unceremoniously to the rim of the storage basket they were sitting on. They passed through the huge reinforced gates of one of the walls and could see troops piling down into bunkers below that were integrated into the giant structures.

"Defences above and below?" Jones commented.

"We started digging in a few years back until their armour started rolling over us, so we started building up!" replied the driver.

"You were there for the defence of the city?"

"What's left of it, Sir, yes."

"So someone got out alive," whispered Jones.

They passed through another wall, and as they did, they could see four ships coming into land and a welcome party waiting for whoever it was.

"That's General Heath, Sir," the man said, pointing to a soldier who would have looked more at home by Taylor's side than in a war room. Their vehicle came to a halt twenty metres back from the welcome party. As they climbed off, they saw General White step off one of the ships and approach Heath. Taylor continued right on up to them, and White quickly turned to address him.

"Colonel Taylor, this is General Heath, US Army."

Heath looked to be in his early fifties and stood eye

to eye with Mitch. His face was pot-holed and rough, as if it had been riddled with shrapnel. He was in fighting shape and wore full Reitech gear, being an almost mirror of Mitch himself, though his helmet was off and revealing his almost bald head that had just a little grey hair either side.

"Of all the places we could have met before, Colonel, I can't think of anywhere I would rather have had you on side if a shit storm comes our way, than right here now!"

Taylor smiled.

I like this General already, he thought.

"We have no more time for pleasantries. Gentlemen, please follow me."

He stopped for a moment and looked to Jones.

"Captain Charlie Jones?"

"Yes, Sir," he quickly replied, with a puzzled expression.

"Follow me also."

With that, the General turned and quickly strode towards the entrance to a bunker that was set into the ground. Jones looked to Taylor for answers, but he had none as they stepped down below the surface. It wasn't long before they were standing around a map of the area in Heath's war room, just as Taylor had been so many times before. He never liked it. He was a field officer and never wanted to be anything more.

"Any moment we should be hearing from General Dupont, who I know you are familiar with."

"Yes, Sir," replied Taylor, "but how, may I ask?"

"We have a number of emergency lines set up directly to key installations around the World. We learnt a lot from the last war, and being in the dark again is not something I want to experience. I was here in Baltimore last time we took a stand here, and I can tell you it wasn't pretty."

Taylor could tell Heath had been a fighting man back then. There was no way he'd sat at a desk during that war, with the way he held himself and talked.

"You gave 'em quite a fight."

"I was a Major back then. When I got out, I had less than fifty men still walking and under my command."

A light flashed on the display beside Heath, and he quickly answered before Taylor could even think of a response to his comment. An image of Dupont was projected, and Taylor could already see the pained expression and pale face of a man who was hanging by a thread. He began to open his mouth but stopped and stared at Taylor.

"You made it?"

"I don't die that easy," replied Mitch.

It brought a smile to Dupont's face and the faintest of hope back to his eyes.

"What can I do for you, General?" asked Heath.

"I am sorry to say, and I must be blunt about this. This is a plea for help. Our lines are crumbling. Our armies in the south have broken and have been scattered to the wind. We are on the ragged edge. Will you come to us in this time of need?"

Heath took a deep breath and sighed.

"General Dupont, I assure you I would give you all that you require, would it be even possible. I cannot make that decision, nor could I rightly weaken the defences here in Baltimore. I am sorry to say it, but we aren't fairing much better. We're digging in to weather this storm."

"Then we are alone?"

"You must be able to get support your side of the water? Where are the Spanish, the British?"

"In the same boat, I am afraid. And many of the UEN nations are in open civil war since the arrival of Erdogan's forces."

Dupont went silent and for a few moments and was close to weeping. He finally looked back at them. "This is like nothing we have faced before. I'm getting reports of technology we have never experienced, and lines are breaking easily. I don't know how much longer this can go on for."

"You just keep up the fight, and we'll do the same. Give them all we've got. Look to your allies. Even now, troops are en route to support us here. When we can, we'll come and help you."

"Thank you, General. One last thing, I asked if you knew the whereabouts of Captain Charlie Jones?"

"Yes, he is here with us now."

Jones stepped up beside Taylor into the view. He looked

suspiciously at Dupont and said nothing.

"Captain, I am sure you would like to have news of your wife. She is safe within the facility here. If you can be directed into private quarters, I can have you put through."

Jones looked at Heath, who simply pointed to a door off to one side.

"Thank you," Jones said and walked cautiously to the room, not knowing what to expect.

The door was shut behind him, and a screen projection displayed before him. It was not Coco, but a doctor he did not recognise.

"Captain Jones?" asked the woman.

He nodded in return.

"I want to let you know that both your wife and unborn child are safe and secure and in good health."

Jones was still silent. The doctor peered into his frozen expression.

"Captain?"

"Child?" he whispered.

"Your wife is nine weeks pregnant," she said.

"I didn't know."

"I'm sorry. I had no idea."

"No...it's okay."

Jones didn't know what else to say.

"The important thing here is that Coco is recovering well and will be able to leave shortly, though, I am not sure where... well... where she can go."

It suddenly dawned on him the danger she was in, and just how far he was from being able to help her. The doctor was as speechless as he was now and looked a little flustered at having been caught in such an uncomfortable position.

"I can put you through to her for a few moments," she quickly added.

He nodded. "Please."

He was still stunned as the screen transitioned to Coco, who was sitting up in bed. She had evidently been waiting for him because she was looking right into his eyes with a smile.

"How are you?" she asked.

It struck him as bizarre. Like they had just woken up in their remote farm without a care in the world. He tried to respond, but his throat was dry. He coughed to clear this throat and finally managed to speak.

"Good...sort of."

Both were quiet, as they tried to think of something to say or someway of asking what they were both thinking. Jones looked away for a moment and then to her as she hung onto his every expression, waiting for him to speak.

"So...you're..."

She nodded and then smiled.

"I know it's not exactly the best timing, and I didn't know until yesterday...but..."

"But nothing, it's the best news I've heard all year."

She was silent once more and began to weep.

"What is it?" he asked.

She tried to wipe away the tears as she replied. "I thought you'd be so mad."

"Why on earth would you think that?"

She sobbed once more. "I don't know."

"I came in here expecting the worst, and I've got the two best pieces of news I could ever hope for, and never for a moment dreamt could be true. We just have to get you out of there. I'll find a way to get to you, don't you worry."

She shook her head, and her face suddenly tightened and became more serious.

"No, you will not."

"What?"

"I'm already out of this fight. I won't have you as well. You have people who need you. Taylor needs you."

"They'll understand."

"No, they'd accept you leaving, but they might not survive it. I'm safe here."

"But..."

"No," she said firmly, "I will not have you leave your post because of me. You will stay there and do your duty."

He wanted to fight her on it, but he could see the determination in her eyes. The door beside Jones opened, and the man who had led him in there poked his head around the corner.

"Sir, I'm sorry, but we need to free up the line."

"All right."

He turned back to her.

"I have to go, but you look after yourself, you hear?"

"I will, look after both of us," she said with a smile, "Good luck, Charlie."

The screen went black, and Jones shook his head in astonishment.

"Stubborn fool," he muttered to himself with a smile.

His mind was reeling as he left the room to join Taylor and the other officers, who he found to be in deep conversation. Mitch could see the look on Jones' face and suspected the worst. Without interrupting the discussion, he looked into Jones' eyes and mimed the words, 'you okay?' Jones shrugged and nodded, but Taylor couldn't tell if he was genuinely okay, or if his stiff upper lip attitude would give the impression he was either way.

"Colonel?"

Taylor hadn't even noticed Heath calling his name.

"Colonel Taylor?"

He snapped out of his concern for his friend and turned to the General; he looked far from impressed by his lack of attention.

"Think you can handle that, Colonel?"

"Yes...yes, Sir."

"I need everyone under my command at one hundred percent, Colonel, so get your head in the game."

He simply nodded in return.

"Then you all know what to do. We're in this for the long haul. Dig deep. We need everything you have got to give. Keep your people together. Keep the morale high, and keep up the fight. That will be all."

Taylor turned and left with Jones. It immediately struck him as strange that his friend did not enquire about what was discussed with the Generals after having missed the entire briefing. His mind was elsewhere. Mitch stopped and put his hand out to stop Jones, who would have gone on not having noticed otherwise.

"Come on, spit it out."

"What?"

"You've got some news, Charlie. It's obviously a big deal. Let's hear it."

"Coco, she's okay, and so is our unborn child."

It was the last thing Taylor was expecting to hear, and he didn't know what to say.

"I know, still can't believe it myself."

"Well...that's great," replied Taylor.

He tried to be convincing, but he couldn't hide the overwhelming feeling he had, that it was the worst timing in the world, and Jones could tell.

"I know. I know what you're thinking, and don't think I don't feel it too. But those are the facts of it, and now we just have to deal with it."

"So what are you gonna do?"

"About what?"

"Your wife is the middle of a warzone, and you're the other side of the World."

"I know that, but she told me to stay. Coco said I had to stay here, and keep doing what we're doing."

"And you don't have a problem with that?"

"Of course I do, but I don't see how I can help. Over there is a war zone, over here is a war zone. Let's grind these bastards down and break them over these walls, and then worry about it."

Taylor was surprised he wasn't rushing off to be by Dubois' side, but he was glad of it.

"So what's the plan?"

"Heath has allocated us an area to defend. It doesn't really get any more complex."

He looked out for the ride that had got them there, but the mule was nowhere to be seen. The crude and utilitarian flatbed transport was luxury, compared to having to walk after the long days they had experienced.

"Great," muttered Taylor.

He stopped for a moment and looked around at their surroundings, realising they were in the remains of downtown Baltimore. A few storefronts made up part of a wall nearby. Cars and brickwork had been piled high beside them, and the whole lot filled with concrete and other materials.

"Looks like a wasteland fortress."

"You know why?" asked Taylor, "Because it is."

He could see the command post had been built from the remnants of a subway station. The city was a continuous layer upon layer of walls, trenches, and barricades. Paths were no wider than a few metres, and the walls every block or two made sure no armoured vehicles could pass within the city limits. Gun towers lay camouflaged within the upper floors of the last remaining floors of tower blocks.

"You know how often in history a fortress like this has ever held out?"

"I know."

"Fortresses like this exist to hold long enough for reinforcement on the ground. Think that kind of aid is coming?"

"We can only hope."

They carried on back to their own unit on foot. Everywhere they looked, troops were digging in, improving defences, or ready and awaiting an attack.

"You have to know this is the worst we've ever had it, Mitch?"

"Yep."

"They hit us when we we're at our weakest, and they hit us harder than ever before. You really think digging in like this is the way?"

"What else can we do?"

"What you normally do when facing vastly superior numbers and firepower. Fall back. Don't take them head on."

"A guerrilla war?"

"Yes," replied Jones.

"The day we do that is the day we accept we have already lost."

Jones said nothing more of it as they continued on. Half the troops they passed were fresh and clean and had clearly not seen action yet. The other half looked like they'd been through several months of combat, not the last few hard days.

"And if this city falls?"

"What about it?"

"Stalingrad, you know your history. You know what happened to the Germans who survived that fight."

Taylor nodded. It sent a shiver down his spine as he remembered what he had read of those events from so many years ago; starvation, and brutal and bitter bloodshed followed by long and painful deaths in prisoner of war camps, with the most atrocious of conditions.

"And if you think they had it bad, you have no idea what this enemy will do to us."

Jones knew all too well, and that made Taylor hold his tongue. Not another word was spoken until they finally found their own ships and people in sight.

"This is it, this is where Heath wants us to stay."

"And the birds?"

"Nowhere safer for them to go than where they are."

Jones shook his head. They both knew it was another sign of bad times. Taylor carried on to towards King and a Grey who stood chatting beside one of the craft. The few hundred troops of Inter-Allied were scattered about, mostly doing little more than resting their weary legs.

"All right, gather around!" Taylor ordered.

Most stayed put and only those further out wandered into hearing distance.

"Our orders are simple! We hold this ground!"

It came as little surprise to any of them.

"For many of us, this means fighting on home soil. But let's not forget we have fought this enemy as one, as one race. So don't think of these as foreign lands for those from across the water. This is Earth. This is your homeland. It doesn't matter where we fight because it's all ours, and that's how it's gonna stay. So who's ready to give those bastards hell?"

He got a few cheers, but it was nowhere near the enthusiasm he wanted.

"I said who wants to give these bastards hell?" he boomed even louder.

Every man and woman of the Regiment roared at the tops of their voices, to the extent it brought most passersby to a standstill.

"Nobody ever won a war by being mopey bastards. They won it by being the go getters, the life takers, and the ass kickers you were all born to be!"

Another roar of excitement echoed around the walls either side of them. Taylor was at least satisfied he had riled them up enough.

"This is our land. This is our castle. Take up positions, and be ready to defend it with every fibre of your being!"

With that, he turned and walked away to a cheer from the troops. He headed for the group of officers who stood awaiting him with Jones at their centre.

"Little over the top, don't you think?"

Taylor shrugged his shoulders.

"It's what they wanted to hear."

Jones muttered something under his breath, and it was clear Taylor's speech had not been his idea of inspiring the troops. Yet he didn't want to admit that it seemed to work.

"Incoming," a voice shouted from the walls above them. The call was being repeated every twenty metres through the base as Taylor rushed up onto the barricade. Hundreds of alien vehicles were approaching. Those tracked were stopped at the lines of traps and barricades that had been built, but skimmers and aircraft continued on.

Huge gun emplacements along the length of the wall opened fire when the first enemy targets came within a kilometre range. Taylor watched, hoping it be enough to bring them down, but even he could see it wouldn't be. A few of the ships exploded, but many more continued on. Pulses from the enemy vehicles soared towards their wall, and Taylor could only duck down into cover and hope for the best.

Thunderous vibrations shook their position, and Taylor felt a little sick from the volcanic like eruptions shaking him about. Two more volleys struck their position before they heard the craft soar overhead. Two were struck by ground weapons and crashed down into the defences and erupted on impact. Taylor got to his feet and looked out across the plain. It was utter chaos, thousands of Mechs advancing on the city and drones out ahead of them in skirmish lines.

He could see swarms of enemy craft on the horizon. He looked across the wall to those standing with him. Jones stood shoulder-to-shoulder with US Army personnel. They were speechless. The battle had only just begun, and yet they could see little hope of victory in sight. No one said a word, but Taylor knew he must. He turned and looked at all the stunned and distraught faces of who fought with him.

"You see them!" he shouted.

It grabbed plenty of attention, as no one else had anything to say.

"You've fought them before! You've beaten them before! You think you're scared? Every army they have sent to this world has been destroyed. So it's no wonder how they feel."

Many of them nodded their heads in agreement.

"And here we stand, still alive, still fighting. We are what broke all who came before them, and now they face us? They aren't to be feared. The Krys soldier is nothing better than you. He fights without thought or conviction. He fights because he is told to. You fight because it is your duty, and don't you forget it!"

He looked to Jones who still shook his head, but he continued anyway.

"We can beat these bastards! You can beat them. Run them into the ground and finish this once and for all. Erdogan and his armies are all that stands between the peace we have fought so hard for. Let's not give in at the final hurdle!"

He looked back over the wall. The Mech forces we advancing rapidly now, and the gun towers were taking aim and preparing to fire.

"Do not fear death, for it will come to us all one day. Fear defeat! Are you ready to beat these alien bastards?"

Cheers rang out across the line as the gun emplacements opened fire. He didn't need to say another word as troops rushed to the walls to take up positions. The multi-layered platforms gave them three battlements, and Taylor stood atop the highest. Only Jafar stood taller two metres to his side. Taylor gestured for him to come closer, and he quickly obliged. Jafar looked calmer than any of them.

"No bombardment, an immediate assault? Why would they do that?" Taylor asked him.

"Because they are confident of victory," he quickly replied, without pausing for thought.

"They think they're gonna just roll over us?"

Jafar nodded.

"Well, they're welcome to think it, but we ain't going down without a fight."

"So you would die rather than admit defeat? And yet you always ask me why Mech warriors advance without care or caution or regard for their lives. You seem surprised their morale is so hard to break, when you encourage the same in those you command."

Taylor had to think about it for a moment. What he said made perfect sense, and yet it had never occurred to him before. He looked back at the enemy troops advancing. Many were carrying large shields, not unlike they themselves used.

"This Erdogan, he isn't like our enemies of the past. He is not blindly arrogant."

"No," Jafar agreed.

"He's justifiably arrogant," Taylor added with a smirk.

He took aim with his rifle and watched as the first web rounds launched off from nearby marksmen. He was out of the ammunition himself, so simply left others to it. He stopped for another moment and looked at the spectacle before him. Mech warriors advanced in loose formations. Many clung to hovering armoured vehicles that were spaced ten metres or more apart and mixed among them.

Their advance against the walls of Baltimore appeared archaic in tactics, and yet there they were, still moving forward.

"Fire at will!" he shouted.

He knew they would anyway. Not one of them could stand and do nothing as the weight of a Mech army bore down on them. He took aim at the nearest creature. It bore a large shield like he had seen on the Mechs aboard the Earth Defence Grid. He squeezed the trigger and watched as his shot ricocheted off the corner of the door-sized shield. He shook his head and fired off two more shots, but both seemed to have little effect.

"That's gonna be a problem."

An automatic grenade launcher spun into action on a tower to his left flank. Explosions began rippling through the advancing enemy, tossing Mechs into the air and ripping through the rear armour of many of the shield bearers. A fixed gun on the wall to his right, which was a large Reitech fixed emplacement gun, joined the fight. Its rate of fire was as slow as a steady heartbeat, but each shot tore apart the shields it struck and punched holes in the vehicles they were sheltering beside.

"More like it."

He caught sight of a few Mechs without shields and quickly opened fire, cutting down one with a burst from his rifle. The weight of gunfire hammered the enemy like a torrential downpour. Their lines were being thinned, but they kept coming.

"We need to upgun!"

"No shit," replied Jones sarcastically.

They kept up the fire as the enemy closed half a kilometre on them. There seemed no way of stopping them besides the physical barricade itself.

"What are they thinking?"

"They must have some way in," Jones answered.

Pulses soared over their heads, and some pounded into the walls close to them, but had little effect against the hard cover they were protected by. The Mechs were just two hundred metres away now, and the hovering vehicles among them began to speed up and make a break towards the wall.

"What the hell?" Taylor asked.

Gun turrets atop each of the vehicles continued to fire at the battlements with little effect other than keeping heads down.

"Where are they going?"

"They aren't coming over the wall. They're going through it!" Jones shouted, "Take them out!"

Scores of troops opened fire on the vehicles. As one of the towers opened up, it tore one apart, and it ignited into a raging fire, but it was too late for the rest. Taylor watched in horror as three-metre wide corkscrew-like drills deployed at the front of the vehicles, ready for impact.

"Oh, shit!"

It was too late. They felt the impact as one of the skimmers smashed into the wall at the very base below them. Taylor and several others lost their footing and crashed against the barricade. As Taylor regained his faculties, he could make out the ear splitting sound of drilling beneath them for twenty seconds, and then it stopped. He looked to Jones who stared at him, waiting with suspicion.

The two of them looked over the edge in towards the city, confused. It had gone quiet along the walls. A soldier nearby began to laugh. "They can't get through!" He jumped up onto the top of the rampart and screamed, "Fuck you, you failed!" Jones shook his head.

"This was no accident...they're..."

He was cut off by a massive explosion further down the line, which shook the foundations of the wall and sent huge chunks of concrete hurtling into the air.

"It's gonna blow!" Jones shouted.

He grabbed Taylor, and they rushed to the edge of the rampart, jumping as the explosion erupted in the wall below them. The blast launched them twenty metres through the air. As they hit the ground, Taylor rolled over and saw a five-metre chunk of concrete fly past his head, missing him by only half a metre. He was stunned by the impact, but his suit had at least slowed his descent and broken his fall. He was sitting on the ground before two layers of the fortress that was Baltimore. His shield and rifle were gone, and he looked out to where the wall had been. The area was engulfed in a ball of dust and smoke.

Through the smoke came silhouettes, and they were not human.

CHAPTER FIVE

Taylor was still flat on his ass as the Mechs bore down on the scattered survivors. They lay among the bodies of those killed in the blast, and as the dust began to settle, it became clear the outer wall was slighted. He felt helpless for a moment, coming to terms with what they faced. Then he felt something brush by him. Dozens of troops rushed past towards the enemy, with Captain King at the lead. They fired on full auto as they advanced, but much of the fire was absorbed until they reached the first wave, drawing their Assegais as they went in to hand-to-hand.

He scrambled to his feet to join the fight. As he ran forward, he knelt down and grabbed a shield that lay scattered on the ground before him and the enemy. King had driven right through the first line of Mechs and was already engaging the second with a few of his Rangers. Further waves took on the enemy's first line. Taylor reached the first, and he jumped, using a little power of his suit to launch himself up and over the hulking shield of one of the Mechs. He drove his Assegai into its head.

As he descended, he felt the Assegai pull. It was stuck in the creature, and he was forced to spin to wrench it from the Mech, forcing him to land hard on one knee. He straightened his leg but felt an impact on his shield. It brushed off just enough to push him aside but not knock him over. He looked around and saw a wounded Mech soldier that had been thrown his way. Without hesitating, he leapt onto it and stabbed it three times before it could recover.

He looked up from the ground. There was a never-ending stream of the enemy, and a volley of pulses surged towards them from the nearest soldiers. He raised his shield, watching as much of the energy dissipated over his shield.

"We can't keep this up!" King called out to him.

King turned back to carry on the fight but was struck by a shield edge to the head which buckled his legs. His attacker pulled back its Assegai-like weapon to lunge and finish off the Captain, but Taylor leapt forward, using his body weight to knock the creature onto its back. He repeatedly stabbed it until it stopped resisting. He dropped his shield and holstered his Assegai.

"Cover me!" he ordered Jones and the others fighting with him.

Taylor picked King up. He was barely conscious and muttering something which was indecipherable. He turned back to Jones. He was waiting for Taylor's order.

"Let's get the fuck out of here!"

Without another word, he turned, slung King onto his shoulder, and rushed for the next wall of the defences. The few small gates were flooded with troops trying to retreat. He knew he had no choice but to try and clear the wall. Pulses rushed past him and smashed into the wall, and as much fire was being returned from friendly positions. He looked up for just a moment to find a gap in the friendly firing solution and jumped.

The wall was fifteen metres high and easily manageable by him, but he had no idea if he could make it with the weight of King on his shoulder. He left the ground and hoped for the best. As he reached the upper edge of the wall, he came to the limit of his power, clipping the very edge as he tumbled over it. Taylor recovered just in time to land on the far side without injury, lucky to have found an open space amongst the chaos.

He looked down at King. A deep wound span from his face and down his neck, stopping at the shoulder plate of his armour. He was conscious but faint and weak.

"King? Stay with me."

His eyes opened a little further to look at Taylor.

"You're out of this fight, Captain," he said, looking up at the chaos around him. Jones landed beside him, quickly calling out, "Medic!" when he saw King resting in Taylor's arms.

"We're in it deep here, Mitch," Jones said, kneeling down beside them.

Gunfire raged above them, but Taylor was too caught up in the moment to notice. A medic rushed up to them. It was clear few wounded had made it to safety, as the Captain had his complete attention.

"Please lay him down," said the medic.

Taylor was oblivious to his words.

"Sir, please lay him down, so I can help."

Jones smacked the top of Taylor's helmet to get his attention, and he snapped out of the daze.

"Yes, of course," he said, as he released his grip on King.

"Make sure he is well cared for," Taylor said firmly.

"Of course," the medic replied, and he went to work.

Taylor turned and looked back at the wall. It was a near identical fortification as the one that had been destroyed moments before. He quickly leapt into action towards the nearest ramp leading to the second level battlement, where he could get some visibility over the battlefield while still having protection over his head.

"Wait!" Jones called after him.

He carried on until he stood beside the troops who were laying down constant fire from the defences. Taylor looked out through a small loophole to survey the situation. Jones reached him and waited to see what he was getting at.

"Whatever those breaching vehicles were, I can't see any more of them."

"They're sure to be bringing more up," replied Jones.

"Yes, and we'd better be prepared for them next time."

He looked out at the craft they had flown in on. Only one remained intact and was swarming with Mechs.

"Well, we certainly ain't flying out of here."

"You ever thought we would?" Jones asked cynically.

Taylor grunted. He looked back to see most of his unit had made it.

That is at least a relief.

"Put the word out about those skimmers. Next time we see them, I want them blown to high hell before they get within five hundred metres of the wall," he said to Jones.

"I should imagine that is stating the obvious."

"Yeah, well let's be certain, hey?"

Jones nodded and rushed off to do as ordered. Taylor turned back, looking at the progress of the Mechs. They were digging in at the remnants of the first wall now. Gunfire had already settled down from the chaotic frenzy it had been. Jafar stepped up beside him. One side of his face was covered in blood. He had multiple cuts and impacts from shrapnel, but he didn't seem to pay it any attention.

"Have you ever seen those things before?"

He shook his head.

"I have never seen Erdogan's armies go to war."

"Yeah, well you have now, and it ain't pretty."

They heard a vehicle's brakes skid to a halt behind them, and Taylor turned quickly to see General Heath leaping from a vehicle with gun in hand.

"Sir, you shouldn't be here!"

"I'll be the judge of that!" he snapped.

He rushed up to the wall to look out at the devastation with his own eyes.

"Christ, Taylor," he muttered, "We can't afford to lose lines of defence like that."

"I know."

"Next time they come at us we need to be prepared."

"Yes, Sir."

Heath stepped a little closer to Taylor to talk privately.

"We're in deep shit here, Colonel. Deeper shit than I thought possible. Cities are not falling by the day, but by the hour."

"I don't see what we can do about it."

Heath shook his head. "No, other than keep doing what we're doing."

"I don't understand how they got on top of us so quickly. We had no warning of this at all. No time to prepare."

Heath took in a deep breath. "Our experts tell us Erdogan's vessel, that behemoth up there, seemingly created its own gateway. Their fleet literally jumped into the system right on top of the defence grid. We couldn't have seen it coming."

Taylor turned to Jafar and gestured for him to join them, but he hesitated and looked to Heath for permission. Heath sighed at the prospect before calling him forward.

"I don't like working with the enemy, but I am also well aware what you have done for us all. You have my trust because you've earned it, but don't expect me to be so welcoming of your friends."

"These are my friends," he quickly replied, pointing to Taylor and all those around them.

Heath smiled in response, but it was clear he still wasn't comfortable communicating with an alien.

"I know you heard what we were talking about," Taylor said, "You got any light to shed on the tech of that ship?"

"Only rumours," Jafar replied.

"Well let's hear 'em."

"Some said Erdogan had the technology aboard his flag ship to travel as if through space gateways without having to use them. Many thought it was simply a myth created to keep the other Lords in their places."

"Yeah, well I guess not," replied Taylor.

"Why didn't we hear of this sooner?" asked Heath.

"There are many myths in the universe, General, who decides which are tactically important?" replied Jafar.

Heath nodded.

"Yeah, I guess so. Hindsight's a bitch. Anyway, none

of that helps us now. They're here and at our door, so let's focus on the task at hand. There are nine layers of defences to this city, if you can call it that anymore. We just lost the first. Let's not lose another."

Taylor nodded in agreement, although he wasn't confident of their abilities to do so.

"And if we can't hold?" he whispered.

"Can't? You don't strike me as the kind of man who accepts he can't do something, Colonel?"

Taylor couldn't help but agree, but it didn't make him feel any better about the situation.

"Will that be all, Sir?" he asked.

Heath nodded before jumping back down to his vehicle and leaving. Taylor knew he didn't need to be there in person, but he did at least appreciate his commitment to frontline troops. Mitch turned to see Jones. He was sitting propped up against a chunk of concrete and eating from a field ration in a relaxed fashion.

"Thought you hated those things, Charlie?"

"Yeah, almost as much as starvation. So we got any better plan than wait for the next attack and get another kicking?"

"Nope," he replied, taking a seat beside him.

Just as he was getting comfortable, a barrage of heavy pulses smashed into the walls around them.

"Cover!" Taylor bellowed.

He grabbed Jones and hauled him to his feet. They

both ran to the lower level battlements of the outer wall. Pulses smashed into the ground between the layers of the defences, and the troops huddled for cover in every nook and cranny they could find.

"Those are some big guns!"

"No wonder they halted the air attack," replied Jones.

They all watched the bombardment in amazement. It went on for a full ten minutes. It caused few casualties but destroyed many of the supplies and vehicles that could yet have proved very useful. More than anything, it was demoralising to an almost crippling degree.

"You know we're losing, right?" Jones asked Taylor.

Taylor looked around in surprise to see if anyone else had heard, but he knew Jones would not be ill disciplined enough to have said as much if they were able to. The artillery bombardment ensured nobody could hear any words spoken beyond half a metre from their ears.

"How often have things ever looked good for us? We've come back from worse."

"Have we, Mitch?"

Taylor turned to look at his face full on and see if he was being his usual cynical self, or actually being brutally honest. His eyes told the entire story, and it was the first time Taylor worried they could not win the war. His heart sank as it all came home to him.

This truly is the worst it's been, he thought.

"We've barely fought against this new invasion, and yet

you must see where it's going."

"So what, Charlie, we just give up? Was it all for nothing?"

"I didn't say that, but maybe staying to die here isn't the answer either."

The bombardment suddenly stopped. Taylor climbed up to a loophole to get a look out across the plain between them and the enemy lines. He could already see glimmers of movement amongst the rubble.

"Here we go again," he muttered.

"Incoming!" a voice hollered from high above them.

Taylor rushed up to the next level and could dust clouds in the distance. Enemy vehicles were rushing from the coast over the flattened ruins of housing neighbourhoods and parks where nothing had lived for many years. He already knew it would be a repeat of what they had seen earlier, and that he could do nothing now but hope the defenders at the wall were able to take them down, knowing what they now knew.

Jones appeared at his side and pointed up to the sky that was filled with the silhouettes of enemy vessels. They turned and looked back west; friendly aircraft were en route to intercept.

"At least we got air cover," he muttered.

They watched with bated breath as the Mech vehicles soared towards their defences. They had all seen or experienced the horrific destruction of the first line of defences, and it took immense willpower to stand their ground on the second. Taylor readied his rifle. He had no idea if he could penetrate the frontal armour of the vehicles, but he was gonna put everything into them he could.

He looked along the line. Every anti tank weapon and heavy weapon they could muster was positioned ready for the next wave.

But will it be enough?

It wasn't long before the vehicles passed into range, and he could start to make out their shapes through the dust cloud. He held his fire for them to close the distance and watched as the gun towers above him opened fire. The crews took the small armoured skimmers seriously this time and targeted them immediately.

Taylor could see how terrifying the breaching vehicles were to all those around him, and he felt it too. The last one had almost been the end of him, and it made him think of Eli and how much they had to lose. He stood back and looked for her. About ten metres along the line he spotted her, and she was looking at him at just the same moment. It was all the time he could spare, and he went back to his position as the first wall mounted weapons opened fire. Two of the vehicles ahead burst into flames, and one of them veered off course, smashing into another that caused it to flip over and dig itself into the ground and come to an abrupt halt.

Cheers rang out across the line, and Taylor briefly thought they had a chance of stopping them, but the gunfire continued all the same. Their nearest vehicles were now within two hundred metres and closing fast. Taylor took aim and fired three single shots in rapid succession and watched as each one glanced off their armour.

"Not good," he grumbled.

He looked around and wanted to say something. He wanted to call on some reserve, bring something else into play, but there was nothing. Engines roared overhead as Mech flyers soared over them, unopposed by the gun towers that were too occupied on the ground. Mitch looked up at doors opening on the vehicles, and Mechs leapt out, descending onto the open plain before them and throughout the tiers of defences beyond.

"So not good," he said to himself.

He knew he could do nothing against the incoming vehicles, so he turned his attention to the airborne Mechs dropping among them. He targeted one descending near to him and fired a burst into its back, killing it before its feet hit the ground. He turned his attention to another and fired several shots as it landed, but most missed, and only one hit it and glanced off. Remembering the assault beyond the wall, he turned back for just a moment and watched another of the vehicles be engulfed in flames. But out of those flames came two more heading for the wall thirty metres to the west.

The fixed weapon emplacements tracked as quickly as they could, but most of their fire missed the vehicles, and it was too late. They hit the wall with a vicious impact, and just as before, went silent for a moment. Jones froze and looked to Taylor in horror.

"Off the wall!" Taylor screamed.

He immediately ran to the edge and jumped. He had to hope the others would follow suit. Taylor was heading head first onto a Mech and simply slipped his shield beneath his feet like a surfboard and landed square on top of it. The weight of the impact smashed it head first into the ground, but that wasn't enough certainty for Taylor. He landed fairly solidly and quickly put the barrel of his rifle to the back of the Mech and fired a three-shot burst.

"Take cover!" someone yelled.

It was the only reminder he needed. He rolled over and lifted his shield to hide behind it, and had just five seconds before the blast ignited. Showers of debris impacted over his shield, but nothing substantial. He pulled it aside and got up. The wall before him had remained intact, but then he turned westward and could see the dust settling and a gaping hole in their defences. In his daze he had forgotten all about the Mechs dropping above them, and a pulse stuck the ground only centimetres from his feet. He raised his shield, and as he looked up, one of the creatures was hurtling towards him.

The Mech struck the base of his shield. It gave way

and twisted his still recovering arm. He let out a cry in agony, as he felt the pin sharp agony run up the arm as the creature landed beside him. With one swing, the creature swung its pulse cannon around and used it like a club to smash him in the flank while the pain was distracting him. He felt his body fold at the waist, and he dropped to the ground.

As he hit landed, he realised the trouble he was in and pulled his shield around to cover his body. The cannon opened fire, and three pulses struck his shield in rapid succession. He had no idea what to do, for he was pinned down, and the shield wouldn't last out much longer.

The firing stopped, and he carefully peered around his shield. His eyes widened on seeing a foot of the Mech stomping down towards him. He raised his shield at the last second, and the impact forced it onto his helmet with such immense force he was knocked unconscious.

* * *

Taylor awoke to a bumpy ride. He was moving fast and looking at the floor. His vision began to clear, and he could tell he was being carried, but was noticeably higher than any human could carry him. A moment later he was placed down to rest and was able to see the face of his saviour - Jafar.

"How long have I been out?" Mitch quickly asked.

"Too long!" a voice yelled at his flank.

He turned and saw Jones bandaging up a superficial wound on his own arm.

"Really, how long?" Taylor insisted.

"Couple of hours."

Taylor's eyes widened.

"Two hours? What the hell has happened in that time?"

"About what you'd expect."

Taylor shook his head. He was relieved to be alive, but the sensation was overwhelmed by his anger that he had not been there to fight the battle. He looked around at the subway station a little over fifty metres ahead of him. It was where he had been called to Heath's operations room.

"What are we doing here? Why aren't we in the fight?"

"We've been pulled back for a little R&R," replied Jones.

"How much have we lost?"

Jones went quiet and looked down as he finished tying his bandage.

"How much?"

He slowly looked up at Taylor, and he could already tell it wasn't going to be good news.

"To the east and north four tiers, but we still hold them to the south and west."

"Four?" asked Taylor.

He wasn't really surprised but still felt shocked. He went silent, taking in everything around him. He could hear the war still raging in the distance.

"We can't stay here," he muttered.

Jones looked over to him.

"What was that?"

Taylor took in a deep breath.

"You were right. We're losing. Stay here and we all die."

It was loud enough that a number of the troops around him also heard what he had said. It was clear they agreed with him. Taylor looked around for a rifle and soon found one, though he had no idea if it was his. He propped it beside him and used it for leverage to get to his feet.

"Where are you going?" Jones asked.

"To make sure the General knows what's what."

"He ain't gonna like that."

"I don't give a shit. We either get out of here ASAP, or it's over for all of us."

Jones couldn't disagree, so he leapt to his side and followed him on towards the subway station entrance. Taylor passed Parker. She stood talking with her platoon, and he acknowledged her as he stepped beyond. He hadn't even thought to ask after casualties and who of his friends might be dead. The survival of them all was too important to be distracted with anything.

"How you gonna play this?"

"Same way I always do, Charlie."

"Piss everyone off, then?"

Taylor smiled a little in response, but it soon waned at the thought of their present situation.

"Something like that, yes."

The guards let him by without question, for they all knew who he was. As the two of them stepped into Heath's war room, they could feel the tension there. Nobody was speaking, and Heath was sitting back and upright in his chair deep in thought while many of his staff just looked lost and confused. The General had the look of a broken man about himself, and Taylor knew it was the prime time to make his point. He strode up to the General so he might talk privately.

"Sir, we're done here," he whispered.

Heath nodded in partial agreement, but Taylor could see General White approaching to join the conversation.

"If you have something to say, Colonel, then let it out," he stated for all to hear.

Taylor looked up and nodded, thinking carefully about how to word it.

"Well come on," added White.

"This fight, this city, it's over. All we can do by staying here is prolong our deaths."

"You are famed for many things, Colonel, cowardice is not one of them, so don't start now."

"Cowardice!" Jones shouted, "You've got some nerve..."

Taylor lifted his hand and stopped the Captain as he tried to lunge forward in his verbal attack. As he did so, he noticed the enemy advances displayed on the map projection. It was clear their were being encircled.

"Sir, we're being surrounded. We cannot survive this. I'm sure everyone in the room is familiar with a tactical withdrawal. You are all qualified officers, after all?" Taylor asked dryly.

The question was rhetorical, and he knew it would piss White off, but they all remained silent as they waited for more explanation.

"This simple fact is we are in deep shit. I don't have the answers, but I do know dying here, and it won't take long, will not help anyone. I say we get out, and put some distance between us and them."

"We were ordered to hold here, and that's precisely what we'll do. I know following orders is a concept entirely alien to you, Colonel, but let's not forget who is in charge here."

"No, let's not," he replied sternly, looking back at Heath who had still not spoken a word or even acknowledged either of them. As Taylor waited for a response, his senses had begun to recover, and he could smell and taste everything around them. A waft of coffee spread through the air, but more than anything, rank sweat dominated the room. He looked over to Heath. There was a burn mark on the side of his helmet and deep scratches in his armour. He had clearly joined the fight at some stage and smelt as bad as he did.

It all only served to make the entire place even more depressing. There was nowhere to go, nowhere to hide, only a grizzly few hours or days left to survive through.

He wouldn't hold his tongue any longer.

"General Heath. Baltimore is a pit for us to crawl into and die. I won't be a part of it. I won't let my people die here because of a fool's errand. We're out of here, and so should you. You'd better decide whether you want to have our help getting out of here, or if you want to stay here to rot."

White jumped into the conversation furiously.

"We cannot leave. We have a duty to..."

But Heath finally moved and slammed his hand down on the table before him. It was enough of a shock to bring White to a halt. As the officer in command, they all looked to him.

"Baltimore couldn't be defended the first time, and it cannot be defended now. I will not stand to lose everyone under my command for no good reason. We're leaving here, and we're doing it as quickly as we goddamn can!"

General White looked astonished by his statement but did not argue it. Heath took in a deep breath. He looked like a broken man who had finally been given a way out of his misery. He looked across his briefing table and the map displayed on it.

"So where will we go?"

"Washington," a voice replied from a hopeful officer nearby.

Heath shook his head.

"DC? Are you kidding me? New York is a wasteland.

We're getting run out of Baltimore, and you think Washington will be safe? No, no, anyone with any sense bugged out of the capitol as soon as this happened."

He slid his hand across the projection until he reached Pittsburgh.

"Yes, this is it. Clearest route out, enough distance from our current location to make a difference, and we should be able to rendezvous with Army forces there. Pittsburgh was a key point in our lines last time we fought on this soil. I know for a fact that emergency measures will already have several regiments in situ. Let's fight this battle on our terms."

Most around the room nodded in agreement, except for White. The General looked to Taylor. It was not hate in his eyes. He didn't like what Taylor was doing, but he smiled in response, for he certainly appreciated it.

"We've got maybe nine thousand troops in this city. Getting them out is going to be no easy task," said Heath, "We're gonna need an hour to get a plan together, Colonel. You've shown us the way. Now I would ask you to go back to your people, and keep doing what you do best. You're a fighter, Colonel. It is where you belong. We'll find a way out of this."

Taylor wanted to turn and leave, but he could not help but think he wanted a hand in the decisions that could mean life or death for so many thousands of his countrymen.

"Sir, I think I can be vital to the planning of this operation…"

"Colonel Taylor!" White interrupted, "You have your orders. Get to them."

Heath turned and glared at him as well, and he knew he had said all he could say without creating new enemies; and he had enough as it was. Taylor nodded in acceptance.

"Thank you, Sir, and good luck," he said to Heath.

He turned and left with Jones by his side.

"You went easy on them," said Jones as they were leaving the building, "Going soft in your old age?"

Taylor stopped and looked at Jones.

"Honestly? My head hurts. My whole body hurts. Standing in there, all I wanted was to get out here and take a breath of fresh air, or as fresh as we can get. Just because I had one idea, doesn't mean I'm full of them. We have always been fighters in this war. We're field officers, nothing more. Let's stick to what we're good at."

They carried on back to their unit. They were getting what rest they could while scattered around the centre of the city. Parker was the first one to approach and had tears in her eyes.

"We're not getting out of this one, are we?" she asked, standing in front of them.

Taylor righted himself and stood proud with a stern expression on his face.

"When have we ever not got out? We are getting out,

and we are winning this war, and don't you forget it!"

CHAPTER SIX

Taylor looked out to the south at the Mech forces encircling the city. He was on top of the tallest tower still remaining and could see kilometres into the distance, but it was also a rather disconcerting feeling, like being in a fishbowl. He couldn't help but feel the enemy could take a pop at him at any moment. He climbed onto the ladder, slid down to the next level, and walked out onto the wall where Jones was waiting.

"Not nice up there, is it?"

Taylor shook his head. Engines fired up behind them, and he looked down at the vehicles being prepared to leave. Every road and airworthy vehicle still in the city had been gathered ready for the retreat, but he wondered if it would be enough. He could still hear gunfire in the distance. The troops there were continuing to hold back the enemy.

"Think this plan can work?"

"It has to, Charlie. It's that or die."

"You know what gets me, why haven't they just nuked us yet? Or whatever super weapon they have like it. They could finish us easily while we're all held up here. One day, and we'd be done for."

"Not like they're doing a bad job as it is," replied Taylor.

Although he shook his head even as he said the words, it didn't make sense to him either. Jones took a deep breath and then finally came out with some history, as he so often did.

"You know what Hitler once said, that he would do what Napoleon could not?"

Taylor turned and waited for the punch line.

"He wanted to cross the English Channel, invade Britain, and defeat Russia. He wanted the whole world to know he was a better man and a better leader than those who had come before him. It's no different here. Erdogan wants us all to know he can achieve all that his peers failed, and in record time."

"You think that's really it? All this because of what, pride?"

"Is it that surprising? Jafar says that Earth for them is some paradise, so maybe they don't want to use apocalyptic weapons, but I'd bet good money that's not the case. Erdogan is revelling in the fact he is running circles around us. We know he's targeting you personally.

You are a symbol of the human resistance and the defeat of the Krys armies. I'd bet any money he'll be looking to fight and kill you in person."

Taylor couldn't help but laugh.

"Well, you are full of good news. So this ultimate alien badass has come all this way to personally humiliate me until he can finally kill me with his own hands?"

Jones nodded.

It had the ring of truth about it, but Taylor did his utmost to brush it off as a far-fetched theory. A light flashed on one of the comms boxes along the wall, and Parker quickly answered. She was on the line for just a few seconds when she put the receiver down and rushed over to Taylor and Jones.

"Enemy forces are encircling the city fast. We are ordered to get moving now!"

Taylor looked out across the courtyard and quickly yelled at the top of his voice, "Load up. We're outta here!"

He immediately jumped from the edge and landed down beside the vehicle that had been prepared for him. It was an open top jeep, and with nothing but a roll cage for protection. A door gun from one of their ships had been hastily fitted on the cage. Parker climbed onto the back, and Taylor jumped into the driver's seat. Jafar hauled himself into the passenger side. He was so tall his head stuck up above the cage. He had the same weapon across his lap as was bolted to the frame above. Taylor fired up the engine.

"We're not waiting?"

"For what?" Taylor asked.

She was surprised to see him be so eager to leave without checking on those under his command.

"We wait for nobody. We have a duty to get out of here, and to survive to fight another day. We're hitting the road."

He put his foot to the floor, and the vehicle raced out through an archway and past a line of vehicles with troops hastily boarding. Small aircraft were taking off through the base, and he wished they could be aboard one, but they had no such luck. He leaned a little towards Jafar.

"Jones has a crazy theory that this Erdogan bastard wants to bring me down. That he wants me to have my whole life torn apart, and then kill me him very self. That sound like something he would do?"

"I have never met the Lord Erdogan. But yes."

Taylor was shocked and turned to look at Jafar's face. He looked back to see a vehicle pull across their path and swerved just in time to miss it.

"Whoa, what the hell?" Parker squealed as she held onto the roll cage.

Taylor ignored her and asked Jafar again.

"In all this war, a war of whole worlds, you think he wants to make me personally suffer?"

"Yes."

Taylor shook his head because Jafar was being far from descriptive, and yet he quickly realised he was saying all he needed to. Taylor suddenly felt very vulnerable and more than a little uncomfortable. It was a grim feeling to know the most powerful being known to them in the universe was coming for him.

"He's gonna find me, isn't he? Somehow, somewhere, not so far from now, he's gonna find me?"

"Yes," replied Jafar.

Taylor had run into most situations with the utmost confidence, even if it was foolish to do so, but now he doubted himself.

"Make me a promise, Jafar?"

The alien looked surprised and awaited a response.

"Promise me that when the time finally comes, when Erdogan is standing before me and attempting to end my life, you will be beside me trying to finish this."

"I will," he quickly replied.

He seemed to show no concern and fear for the request, but it was still difficult to read his expression.

"You think you could beat him in a fight?"

"No."

Taylor smiled. "Well that's good news."

Deep down it was a horrifying concept. Everyone he knew treated him as some unbeatable champion, but he knew he had beaten Karadag and Demiran with help and a lot of luck. He'd never admit it to anyone, only perhaps

Eli in his weakest moments, but it weighed more heavily on him now than ever. Erdogan was a new kind of enemy on an entirely different level, and it was quickly becoming clear to them all.

A line of vehicles raced out in front of them, and they were losing a little speed as the choke points started filling up.

"There are gates every hundred metres on every wall, and yet still we're getting backed up. This isn't going fast enough!" Parker complained.

It was clear to Taylor she hadn't heard any of the discussion with Jafar, and he was glad of it. Out of nowhere a pulse smashed into the vehicle ahead of them. It was vaporised and most of the body flattened into the ground. Taylor swerved quickly, and the front wheel hit part of the wreckage, launching one side of the vehicle into the air before smashing back down with a violent impact.

Taylor barely kept a grip on the wheel and was amazed they were still going forward, but before they could appreciate their luck, another few pulses struck the ground around them. Engines roared overhead; it was Mech ships sweeping by.

"This isn't good," muttered Taylor.

They were almost bumper-to-bumper with the vehicles ahead of them and had to simply hope the line kept moving. They passed through another archway without incident, but pulses were smashing into positions a little more than ten metres away.

"Erdogan will be watching and revelling in this," stated Jafar.

Taylor looked at him in surprise. Not by what he said, but the fact he had openly shared information without being pressed for it.

"Go on," Taylor said.

"We're running. Fleeing from his armies. Fleeing from his superior power."

"Yeah, well he can stuff his superiority up his ass because I'll be coming for him before long."

Jafar nodded but did not reply. They could all see it was every man and woman for himself now as vehicles scrambled to get out of the city.

"He could have finished us here. He could have ended it all, but Erdogan's arrogance will be his undoing."

"Unless his arrogance is founded in fact!" Parker joined in the conversation.

Taylor looked around. She was hunkered down in the vehicle and just behind them.

"We aren't going down without a fight," he told her firmly.

Neither of them replied. Taylor looked back. Jones' vehicle was close behind them and nearly identical to his. He looked up at more ships flying past overhead, and Mechs were leaping from them and descending into the city. One of the Mech warriors was heading right for Jones' vehicle. He put the power down to get clear and nudged the back of Taylor's jeep. The creature clipped the back of the cage on Jones' vehicle and bounced off onto the front of a truck behind. Taylor breathed a sigh of relief, but as he looked back to the road ahead, he could see further Mechs dropping down ahead of them.

"Get on that gun, Parker!"

She wearily got up on the back of the vehicle and took aim, but it was Jafar who fired first. He had the gun in his lap and could do little to aim, but started firing and adjusting his angles. The first burst zipped past a Mech, and he simply held down the trigger and tracked with the tracer fire until the shots tore into the creature's armour.

"Not bad!" Taylor smiled.

Jafar went on to the next target without responding. As they passed through another layer of the city's defences, they could see they were now heading for the final barrier, and the open area between them was awash with burning vehicles and debris.

"Almost there!" he added.

Parker turned and began to fire rapidly towards a group of Mechs landing nearby while Jafar fired in the opposing direction. Taylor could see that several Mechs were coming down on the convoy ahead of them. He raised his rifle to fire single-handed, but before he could, one of the creatures fired. The pulse struck a soldier in the vehicle ahead of him. The impact went down his helmet and into the neck, killing him instantly.

The body fell off the vehicle and to the ground ahead of them. Taylor wanted to swerve, but there was no room to manoeuvre. They hit the body square on and could hear the gut wrenching sounds of the body striking the axles and wheels as they ramped over part of the body. Another Mech suddenly dropped onto the vehicle in front and bounced off the cage so that it was thrown into their path.

Taylor fired a burst as it hurtled towards them, but there was no way to avoid it, whether it was dead or alive. The creature's arms stretched into the crew compartment, but the middle bar of the cage stopped it dead. It quickly tried to reach for Taylor, but Jafar kicked its faceplate. It shattered and was driven back. Jafar put the barrel of his weapon to its head and fired a burst at point blank range.

Blue blood spurted out over the cockpit in the moment of overkill, forcing Taylor to lean out over the side to see where they were going. Jafar stood up, grabbed hold of the dead body with both hands, and shoved it off the vehicle.

"What I wouldn't give for a roof!" Taylor hollered and sat back in his seat properly. As he said it, they burst out of the final wall and into the open plain to the west.

"On the home run now!"

He could see dozens of vehicles in front of them, and a dust cloud beyond where others were ahead. Just as he spoke, a friendly copter plunged into the ground twenty metres from them and slid to a halt before catching fire. He didn't want to think of how many souls were aboard. The gun above him opened fire again, and he saw Parker firing at an incoming ship. Several of the shots ripped holes in its underbelly, forcing it to bank sharply.

"How long have we got?" she shouted out.

"Soon as the last vehicle hits the three klick marker!" he replied.

"Three klicks? Cutting it a bit fine, don't you think?"

He simply nodded in response. He looked down at the speedo, and they were doing sixty kilometres an hour, the most they could manage and stay in a straight line over rough ground. Taylor looked back at the few dozen or so vehicles behind him and many more on their flanks. They appeared to be close to the rear.

"Masks on, suit up, and buckle up!" he ordered.

He knew they didn't have long now. He slid the visor shut on his helmet and pulled the harnesses across from his seat. The vehicle was fortunately designed for high-speed off-road work and was equipped as such. He sure was glad not to be in the back of one of the trucks.

"Think Heath will really push the button?"

"Bet your ass he will, Parker. Look at it, wouldn't you?"

"What are our chances of survival from a nuclear blast at three kilometres?" Jafar asked.

Taylor shrugged. "It's the minimum distance at which survival is a possibility."

"Oh, great!" Parker sighed.

With that, he put his foot down a little further on the accelerator. He could feel the steering was incredibly light, and they were more skimming over the surface than actually gripping it. The slightest of impacts could send them into a spin, but he hoped for the best, noticing all those around him were doing likewise. Parker looked back through a scope on her rifle at the enemy ships swarming over the city.

"We could never have held it, never should have been there to begin with."

"Easy to say now," Taylor added quietly.

He could see they had easily gone past the marker and were still storming west, but he did not lift off the pedal. He was counting seconds in his head now, trying to calculate how far from the marker they had got. But as he reached forty-four seconds, a quick flash lit up the skies, and he knew it could only be one thing.

Oh shit!

He looked back for just a moment and watched the fireball rise into the sky. He noticed how Parker was frozen solid and staring at it. He could see the shockwave advancing rapidly towards them and looked back at the road ahead, still hoping for the best. He saw Jafar duck and brace for impact. It was a few seconds later the impact struck, and their jeep immediately turned and went into a spin before hitting an embankment and flipping over.

They rolled countless times until finally coming to a standstill on the roof of the roll cage.

No one moved for a moment. They were all stunned by the impact. None of them knew what to do, as they tried to work out if they were still alive. Taylor finally reached down for his harness strap and released it. He dropped onto the ground with no finesse at all. He went straight for Parker without any care for his surroundings. She was motionless, but as he climbed into the back of the vehicle, he could see her eyes were wide open and she was frozen in shock.

Taylor tapped on her mask a few times, and her eyes eventually turned to the sound of the impact and then to him, but they were still wide and her face was pale.

"We made it," he said.

She didn't respond. He unclipped her belt and supported her weight. She fell into his arms, and he lifted her out from the overturned jeep. Jafar began climbing out. Taylor laid Parker down beside the vehicle before turning to look back at the city. A vast mushroom cloud engulfed it. It was all he could make out. Before him lay dozens of vehicles which had been halted by the blast. Many were overturned, and several had collided with each other. A few bodies lay strewn around where occupants had been thrown from the vehicles, although most had been saved by their equipment and were being helped to their feet. Jafar stood next to Taylor, staring at the desolate scene.

"The gloves are off now," Taylor said, "Pride may have stopped Erdogan from ending us in the city, but now we've used a nuke against him, God knows what he'll throw at us."

"Not if he wants you."

Taylor thought about it for a moment.

The prospect of Erdogan hunting me down to end my life is terrifying, but is it saving the lives of hundreds of thousands, maybe millions? Is the alien's pride buying us time? Taylor wondered.

Jafar turned and walked to the vehicle. He placed his hands on the roll cage and shoved it over. The lightweight vehicle sprung over and landed hard on its wheels.

"Time we got out of here," said Taylor.

He could see troops scrambling to get back on the road, and numerous vehicles were already in motion. Many had soldiers piled high as they abandoned their wrecks. Two approached, and Taylor quickly recognised one as Rains and the other as Lang.

"Come on, jump in!"

As they piled in, another two soldiers he did not recognise clambered onto the side and squeezed into the only gaps they could find. Taylor pulled away but without the same sense of urgency they'd had previously.

They carried on at a comparatively casual pace, compared to the frantic rush they had experienced before. He could see the radiation warnings flashing in the display of his visor, but he had to keep faith in his suit to protect him from the radiation, for nothing else would.

They travelled all the way to Pittsburgh without another word between them. Not even the strangers who had jumped aboard muttered anything at all. They were shocked by what they had seen. They all understood it was the beginning of a new phase in humanity. Taylor knew that having to use a nuclear weapon to cover their retreat left them all feeling empty.

Taylor hadn't witnessed Baltimore when it stood as a bastion in the first war, but he knew just how it would feel. He thought back to the time he'd first heard of the loss of Ramstein. He hadn't seen that, but it meant to him what Baltimore must have to many of those who had defended it.

Despite the silence, the drive to Pittsburgh passed quickly as they fell into a daze. Taylor was on autopilot, and a hundred thoughts rolled around his head. By the time they reached the perimeter of friendly defences, he was feeling a weakness he had not experienced before. Running never felt good, and he could not help but feel they were moving from one defeat to another.

Is this the endgame?

"So, Pittsburgh? Wasn't it destroyed by the war, too?" Parker asked as they made their final approach.

"No," Taylor quickly replied, "Sure there was some hard fighting here, but it never got like Baltimore. This is seen as the second line of defence for a reason."

"Well let's hope it works better than the first."

Taylor couldn't bring himself to comment, but he felt the same. The were at the back of the convoy when they reached the forward positions at Pittsburgh, and it was clear they were in a long line of forces which had passed through; those stationed there paid them little attention as they went through.

They could see the faces of the defenders there showed the same lack of faith in their chances as those who had fled Baltimore. Taylor was beginning to wonder if it was the beginning of the end.

And yet, we're still alive. It's something.

They soon reached an initial line of well-developed trench works and passed over one of the few bridges across it. He had no idea what they were heading for, but kept driving on and following those in front.

After a while, they started to descend into a small valley with high sides. It was lined with vehicles and was certainly some kind of sheltered gathering point. There was a mobile command truck at the far side, and it seemed like the obvious place to head. He squeezed the jeep down a narrow channel of troops and vehicles until they rocked up outside the truck.

Most of those they passed lay about in a stunned fashion. There was little fight left in them. As their vehicle came to a stop, a guard rushed forward.

"Move it on!" he yelled.

Taylor jumped out and approached the guard square on, with his rank visible on the front plate of his armour.

"Colonel, you cannot park that here, Sir," the man said, but showing a little more respect.

Taylor tried to carry on past, but the guard lowered his rifle into a broad barrier and tracked with the Colonel to block his path.

"Let him through!" a voice bellowed from behind the guard.

The man looked back and saw General Heath at the side door of the vehicle and quickly jumped back out of the way.

"Yes, Sir!" he shouted. He stood to attention and saluted.

Heath was still in his armour, although it was blood stained now, but it couldn't have been his own as he didn't appear to be wounded.

"Glad to see you made it, Colonel. Plenty didn't."

"General White?"

Heath shook his head. "Wounded badly. I can't say whether he'll survive or not."

Heath turned and carried on inside the truck, expecting Taylor to follow him in. Taylor stepped inside and found three of Heath's staff sitting around a table. There was no display on it, and none of them spoke a word.

"Honest truth is pretty obvious for all to see," he said, "So, we're on the run. What are we gonna do about it?"

He was looking directly at Taylor and had obviously already asked the same of the others present, and not received a useful response.

"Gentlemen, we stand at the brink of destruction, and not one of you has a single word to say? Taylor, you've pulled more than a few tricks out of your hat in the last few years; now is the time for a repeat."

Taylor shook his head. "I wish I had an answer, but did you see what happened to us back in Baltimore? They've got air superiority, improved armour and shields, and seemingly infinite numbers of troops to throw at us."

"So what? We just lay down and die?"

"We need help, Sir. We can only punch so far above our weight. We need a few divisions brought in to help."

"I've been made all kinds of promises, but as you might expect, enemy forces are already spreading far in land and holding up any chance we might have of getting any aid."

"Has it really come to this?" Taylor asked wearily, "Have we fought all this time just to be beaten in a few days?"

Heath did not respond.

"I don't have any answers for you, Sir. All I can say is we will keep on fighting."

Taylor turned to leave.

"You know France is close to falling?"

Taylor stopped and looked back in horror.

"Already?"

"France has been at the core of the wars for the last few

years, so it is no surprise the enemy wanted to occupy it quickly. They intend sending out a message to the World, and it will certainly work."

Taylor shook his head and walked out. The guard who had tried to stop him was still glaring at the jeep they had arrived in, but Jafar was leaning against it and glaring back. The guard dared not approach him. The two soldiers who had leapt aboard were gone without a single word. Parker, Rains, and Lang lay about in the back.

"What's the plan?" asked Rains.

"Find the rest of the Regiment for a start."

"Regiment?" Parker sneered, "Hardly."

"If we three were all that remained, we would still be the Inter-Allied Regiment, and always will be while one of us still draws breath. Now let's find our people."

He jumped in the vehicle and headed off without much of an idea where he was heading. He tried to activate the comms channel on his suit, but it was no longer working. "See if you can get someone, anyone," he said to Parker.

"Already tried. I can't pick up any signal."

"They're taking our infrastructure apart. Probably knocked out the repeaters and satellites," Rains joined in the conversation.

Taylor recognised a marine on the road ahead. He was trying to thumb a lift. It was Corporal Herrera. They stopped beside him.

"Glad to see you made it, Colonel," he said.

The Corporal was empty-handed, and a thick layer of dirt and dust was coated across his uniform.

"Know where the others are?"

"Yes, Sir."

"Then jump on and lead the way."

Herrera guided Taylor a few hundred metres to a small housing complex that had only been partly rebuilt and occupied from the previous war. The troops of Inter-Allied lay scattered about gardens, walls, and abandoned civilian vehicles. They stopped outside a show home; it was impeccably clean and furnished. Two guards were sitting casually outside but got up to attention on seeing him approach the front door.

"As you were," he replied and stepped on through.

He carried on into the house to find a near spotless family residence. The walls were recently painted, artwork and mirrors hung on every wall, and fake pictures of a happy family and their pets lay on a sideboard. The only sign of their presence was the dirty footprints of military boots that led from the door to every room in the house. He went into the kitchen where he could see a hive of activity.

All went quiet as he entered, and he noticed Jones at the core of the meeting.

"Well, I'll be damned!"

"Be careful what you wish for," Jones replied.

He walked up to the large dining table where they were

all sitting around. Silva was there, as well as Lieutenant Ota.

"Jackson?" Taylor asked.

Ota shook her head. "Crushed by a Mech before we got out of the city. We couldn't even recover his body."

"Then you will merge his Company with yours, Captain Ota."

The promotion meant little when it was under such circumstances, but she tried to fake a smile and nod in gratitude.

"What's our current strength?"

"Last figure count was two hundred and eight."

"Well now it's two hundred and thirteen."

Nobody replied, and they waited for him to continue.

"We paid dearly to hold that city for as long as we did, and look where it's gotten us?"

"We nuked the fuckers, didn't we?" Silva asked.

Taylor nodded. "Yes, and we can only hope that it made a sizeable impact on their forces, but either way, they'll be coming for us in force before long."

"Orders from General Heath are to dig in along a five kilometre defensive line, and await reinforcement from the 1st and 3rd Marine Divisions and 2nd Armoured. They should sure raise hell when they get here," Jones stated.

Taylor didn't look confident, and Jones didn't like it.

"What is it?"

"I just came from Heath. Chances of reinforcement

are slim."

"What?"

"We aren't the only ones having a hard time."

"Then what are your orders?" asked Silva.

"As Heath said, dig in. That's all there is to do."

The room fell silent until Taylor finally looked to Jones.

"Can I have a word?"

Jones led him to a small office at the back of the house that was empty.

"Can't say that was a great move for morale."

"No, Charlie, but I'd rather them know the truth, and get to terms with it, than leave them hanging onto something which ain't ever gonna happen."

Jones nodded in agreement.

"So what is it?" he asked.

Taylor sighed, as he thought how to explain and even wondered if he should.

"Well, come on, spit it out. I've never known you to hold your tongue."

"Heath told me a few things while I was with him."

"And?"

"And, well...the simple truth is, France is falling. It's been a focus of enemy forces in what he believes is an attempt to make a point. We both know what France meant to us all through the war, and..."

"And Coco is still there..."

"Yes," replied Taylor, "I'm so sorry."

"That's it. That's all the news you've got? You are going to leave me hanging with that grim prospect with nothing more?"

"Sorry, it's all I have, and there's nothing we can do about it."

Taylor turned about to leave but stopped for just a moment.

"Everyone looks exhausted, including you. I'll get watches set, but let's be sure everyone gets the rest they need. I'll take the first watch. You find a bed in this place and get a few hours in."

He left the office and Jones who was still very quiet. Taylor felt awful for him, but he didn't know any words that might console him, for there was nothing good about their situation.

CHAPTER SEVEN

"We're still alive," said Parker.

He looked over and saw she had sat down a metre to his side, and he hadn't even noticed. He was on watch, but there were so many thoughts cycling around his head that he had not noticed her approach. He looked around at their surroundings. It was a dry and mild night, but more than anything, it was peaceful. There was no sound of gunfire and tracers lighting up the sky. The air was fresh and crisp, and for a moment, one could imagine there was no war at all.

The road in front was perfect, and the houses opposite looked as inviting as the one Taylor was sitting outside of.

"Think it's somewhere you could see us living?"

"If you'd asked me a few months back, yeah," she replied.

"And no longer?"

"No, because come tomorrow or the day after that, it'll be as wrecked as everywhere else we have left behind."

He nodded in agreement.

"You should get some rest."

He looked down at his watch. It was true.

"Yeah, about time Jones did his turn."

He got to his feet and strode into the house and upstairs where he knew Jones had gone. He banged on the door.

"Jones, get up!" he yelled.

There came no response.

"Jones!"

Still nothing. Concern overcame him, and he gripped his rifle in one hand and prised open the door with the other. It was empty. The bed sheets were strewn about from where he had clearly been, but there was no sign of movement. He rushed back down into the kitchen where Lang and Fuchs sat chatting quietly.

"Captain Jones, have you seen him?"

"He left about twenty minutes ago," Lang replied.

"Left? How?"

Lang pointed to the back door of the house.

"Ah, shit, and you didn't think there was something a little suspect about that?"

The two of them looked surprised and unable to answer. Taylor knew there was nothing they could have done or known to have stopped him leaving.

"Oh, hell, Charlie," he muttered, "If he comes back,

you let me know," he said a little louder.

"Do you expect him to?"

Taylor shrugged. "No goddamn idea, Lang."

He strode out of the back door and towards the guard standing at the end of the garden. It was one of Lang's men, but he didn't know his name.

"Captain Jones, where did he go?"

"That way, Sir," the man quickly answered, pointing back to the way they had entered the neighbourhood.

"Know where he went?"

"No, Sir."

Taylor turned and rushed back through the house.

"I've got a pretty good idea," he said to himself.

As he approached Parker, she could see the concern in his face.

"What is it?"

"Jones, he's gone."

He stopped for a moment and could hear a vehicle tearing off into the distance.

"Find Ota, and tell her she's in charge."

"Where are you going?"

"To make sure Jones doesn't get himself killed."

Taylor rushed to the jeep they had arrived in and raced on down the road. He could use only blackout lights and markers because of the risk of enemy detection from the air.

"Goddamn you, Jones, you crazy son of a bitch!"

He had no lights to follow and could no longer hear the vehicle ahead. He stopped at the side of the road beside two soldiers standing guard at a crossroads.

"A vehicle just came by, where was it heading?"

One of them pointed. He began to speak, but Taylor raced off without a word. He was looking around in all directions in a desperate hope to find Jones, but there seemed little chance. Then, as he passed a small park, he noticed a line of copters on the green hidden between trees. Camo nets had hastily been thrown over them in an attempt to conceal their presence.

"Gotta be."

He pulled into the park and raced across the grass towards them and soon noticed a little movement. He slowed the vehicle cautiously until he came to a halt and leapt out. He hoped it was Jones, but he had to be cautious. The gaps he had seen in their lines made him wonder how on earth they could defend such a broad line, and the threat of airborne attack was ever present.

Taylor crept up between the trees, and all the time watching. He could see a camo net being pulled from one of the copters. He took cover beside one of the other vehicles and stopped. He waited to see if he could identify anyone, and then he caught sight of another glimmer of movement. A figure was lifting its arms, and he heard the character say, "My baby."

He knew it could only be Rains. Taylor stepped out

from the cover and paced towards them.

"Rains! What the hell is going on here?"

The Lieutenant nearly jumped out of his skin and then froze. A moment later Jones paced around the corner and stopped.

"What are you doing, Charlie?" he asked.

"You know exactly."

It was true. Taylor knew from the moment he told Jones about the state of France there would be no holding him back, but that wasn't a reason to hide the facts from him.

"You know you would do the same. I'm going to get her out, both of them, Coco and our unborn son."

Taylor didn't know how to respond. It would be hypocritical to try and stop him. He looked around to see four of Jones' unit was with them. Lewis, Wood, Evans and Corporal Robinson.

"You can either leave us be, or help us," Jones said calmly.

Taylor looked to Rains.

"Hey, I got a chance to fly. I ain't gonna say no," he responded to Taylor's glaring eyes.

Taylor shook his head. He didn't even know why he'd chased after Jones other than the fact he had slipped out in the night, but he never imagined the possibility of going with him.

"France is gonna be a death trap," he stated.

"Yeah," replied Jones.

"You're gonna need more than five men to pull it off."

"Probably."

"And maybe twenty-four hours. That means leaving our people for twenty-four hours here. A lot can happen in that amount of time."

"Yep."

"Why should I go with you?"

"Because I would do it for you. Because you know how important this is to me. You risked everything to save Parker. I only ask you respect my right to do the same, and support me like I did you."

Taylor thought about it for a moment.

"This would mean going UA again."

"AWOL, you're in the Army now," replied Jones with a smile.

"God knows what we are anymore."

"Inter-Allied."

He nodded in response.

"All right, all right. I'll come. But let's do this right. We get in and out fast. The mission is to get Coco out safely. We do this without casualties. We can't afford any."

"Agreed," Jones replied and reached out his friend Taylor, tapping him on the shoulder.

"So, who else are we taking?" asked Taylor.

"Just us," replied Rains, "With a single copter and a few guys, we've got a chance of getting in and out of there."

"He's right," Jones agreed.

"This just gets better and better."

"So you're in?"

"Yeah, I guess, but this is your mission. You are taking the lead."

"Okay," Jones replied, somewhat surprised. He looked over to Rains. "How long till we can get this bird in the air?"

"About a minute. She's ready to go."

"All right, then let's move out."

They climbed aboard as Eddie went to the cockpit and fired up the engines.

"So you got much of a plan?" Taylor asked.

"France may be a sinking ship, but she ain't down yet. I figure the lines will be all over the place. A single copter doesn't pose a threat to anyone and shouldn't draw any attention. We head right for Meaux and attempt to put down there.

"Right on top of the base?"

"Yes."

"Which is almost certainly under attack?"

"Yes, well I didn't say it would be easy. Let's just get there and see."

"Great plan," Taylor replied sarcastically, "and how do you know you will have a son?"

"I just know," he said, smiling.

A few moments later they were lifting off in the darkness. Rains was flying by night vision only and with no lights of any sort. It was dangerous, but less so than announcing their presence to all around them.

"You know what really pisses me off about all this?" Taylor asked of Jones.

Jones looked puzzled. "I thought it was a little obvious."

Taylor shook his head. "No. The fact that everything we do is reactionary. Not once have we gone on the offensive. Not once have we forged a plan which isn't merely in a desperate response to what is being thrown against us."

"I don't see how we can do differently. Look at this war. It's a fucking disaster."

Taylor's face tightened as he looked scornfully at Jones. Never did he accept such talk in front of the troops, and yet he relaxed, realising it was both true and unavoidable.

"We're doing this, aren't we? Going out on our own free will to get Coco."

"Who would be perfectly safe if our armies in France were holding out," replied Taylor, "Let's think about this for a minute. We get Dubois out of France, but what then? Where do we go?"

"I don't see what you mean."

"France is falling, I get that, but the United States seems to be following her. We can only retreat so far."

Jones nodded in agreement and put his head in his hands, thinking about it for a moment.

"Earth's a big planet. We'll find somewhere to go," he finally responded.

"Not big enough to hide forever."

It was a grim reality that none of them wanted to face.

"We've got to get back to our unit after this though, right, Sir?" asked Lewis.

Taylor nodded.

"If one thing is certain in this life, it's that we need each other. Inter-Allied will stand together in victory or death."

"Better be victory then, hey?" asked Jones with a smile.

They carried on through the night with no idea of their surroundings. They remained silent and listened for some sign of attack, but it never came. It wasn't long before the sun was up as they passed into new time zones, and morning turned to mid afternoon as they approached the English Channel. Taylor strode up to the cockpit to look out with his own eyes.

"I don't like this. It's way too quiet."

"Can't we just enjoy a bit of peace?" asked Rains.

"Love to, trust me."

"Trust you? Says the man who leads me to hell every time he's in trouble."

"Don't pin this one on me. This is Jones' doing, and you obviously didn't take much convincing."

"Hey, there's a damsel in distress, how could I pass up the opportunity to rescue her?" replied Rains rather jovially.

Taylor could never tell whether Rains was genuinely that calm and relaxed, or if it was a coping mechanism, but it was comforting, no doubt.

"Okay, we got something up ahead," Rains said, looking at his scanners.

"What is it?"

"It's not good, whatever it is. Multiple contacts and they are not friendly."

"Got any ideas?"

"Well, we ain't fighting 'em, and that's for sure."

They banked hard and headed north for the Channel.

"Are they coming after us?" Taylor asked.

"Uhhh....yep."

"Fuck, how many and what are they?"

"Looks like a single fighter coming after us."

"We got any weapons at all?"

Rains shook his head. "She ain't nothing but a transport."

"What do we do?"

Taylor looked around, and Charlie was now standing behind him.

"This is your mission. You're in charge here," replied Taylor.

Jones stopped to think for a moment.

"They're closing on us," stated Rains, "so think fast!"

"Put out a message on all channels. Colonel Taylor of Inter-Allied calling for immediate assistance."

Rains turned around in surprise. "It won't reach anyone but the enemy. We can only communicate short range with their jamming."

"I'm well aware of that, Lieutenant."

Rains quickly understand and conveyed the message across all open channels.

"Dangerous game you're playing here," Taylor whispered to Jones.

"Yeah, just playing on your celebrity status."

"So you just announced to the enemy the man they want dead most in the World is aboard this ship that has no defences? Good move."

"Hey, you said I'm in charge. Let me take the reins."

Taylor backed off, and Jones looked back to Rains.

"Repeat the message. If they fire directly at us, deploy countermeasures, but as late as you can. Then power down and fake engine failure."

"I can do that," Eddie replied with a smile.

He put out the message once again, and immediately a warning light flashed on the cockpit.

"They're trying to knock our engines out. This is gonna be close," said Eddie.

He moved his hand up to the emergency countermeasures button and held his finger just millimetres over it. His hand was shaking a little while he watched the scanner.

"Almost, almost..."

He quickly hit the button, and they felt the copter rock as the explosion erupted just behind them. Jones was knocked about the cockpit but managed to hold on to a rail above Rains. The pilot quickly reached forward and powered down the engines to emergency only.

"That's it. We're on backup power in a controlled descent. We'll be on the ground in about a minute."

"No we won't," Jones said firmly.

He turned back to the crew compartment.

"We've got guns aboard, so we just need to see the whites of their eyes."

"That should be my line, should it not?"

Jones smiled at Taylor. "Get ready."

He raised his rifle and stepped up to the side door.

"Think they'll be stupid enough to come this close?" asked Robinson.

"Damn right! They'll want visual confirmation Taylor is on board, and to be sure nobody bails out."

"They're closing fast!" Eddie shouted out.

"You just tell us when they get parallel with us," Jones said calmly.

"Yeah, whatever you say."

"And be ready to get on the power."

They waited in silence, and Jones could feel the sweat dripping down his face. He prayed the plan would work but knew it was a gamble, like so many others.

"When I open that door, you fire like hell," he said.

"That's your plan?" Taylor asked.

He only stared back.

"Okay, okay."

"They're coming alongside us!" Rains hollered.

"How close?"

"About twenty-five metres!"

"All right, we're in luck. You ready for this?"

They all nodded in agreement as they stood in a firing line beside the door.

"We've only got one shot at this, so you make sure they don't fly again...three...two...one!"

He hit the door release, causing it to quickly slide across and reveal the alien fighter matching their speed alongside them.

"Fire!"

All six of them stood side-by-side and opened up on full auto. Several dozen shots had peppered the hull of the ship that was little larger than their copter. The engines quickly fired, but as it began to move away, they kept up the vicious barrage of fire into the rear of the ship's engines. A small explosion caused fragments to break off the rear hull, and smoke began to belch out.

"Get us moving!" Jones shouted.

Taylor was still firing, looking back until the craft passed beyond range. They both took a look out of the door. It was diving towards the sea and finally plunged into the water. Jones hit the door button and slumped back down into a seat with a sigh of relief.

"Not a bad plan," said Taylor.

Jones nodded in agreement. "Improvise and overcome,

is that not what you always said?"

"Bet your ass."

Taylor went back to the cockpit and looked out once more. In the distance, he could see dozens of black shapes on the horizon.

"What the hell are they?"

"That's the enemy," replied Rains in surprise.

"That far north?"

He turned around. "Britain must be under attack if they're this far north of France."

"I'd be astonished if she wasn't," Jones said.

"And you can live with that and keep doing your job?"

"I wasn't aware it was our job we were doing here?"

"No, but you know what I mean."

The other Brits all looked to Jones for answers, as they were all clearly anxious.

"War is on all over the World. Doesn't matter where we fight, just that we win," he replied.

Taylor gestured for Jones to come up to the cockpit. He obliged but groaned as he got to his feet.

"What is it?" Jones asked.

Mitch leaned in close and spoke quietly.

"All this we're doing, all of it to get your family out of a warzone. What about theirs?" he asked, pointing over to troops who had come with them.

Jones was stunned and speechless. Taylor could already see a little shame in his eyes for thinking only of himself.

"They have given everything for us, everything for you. Shall we not pay it back in kind?"

Jones coughed to clear his throat.

"What have you got in mind?"

"Their families, all those of the Brits amongst the Regiment, they all lived on base, right?"

"Near enough."

"Then that's where we're heading, once we've done our job."

"That's probably fifty families. What are we gonna do with them?"

"We'll find a ship, and we'll make it happen."

"And when we get back to Pittsburgh? We'd be spiriting them away from one warzone, only to take them to another."

"But it would give them hope, something which is sorely lacking, right now."

Jones shook his head. "It's crazy."

"So is flying half way across the World to rescue one women and her unborn child."

He couldn't disagree. "All right, all right."

"Then you tell them."

Jones nodded in agreement and turned back to the others.

"You've gone far beyond what I could ever, or should ever have asked of you. I do not doubt many more among our Regiment would have given it their all, but it is you four who are here with us. You are helping me to save my family, and I intend to return the favour."

"What do you mean, Sir?" Wood asked.

"I mean I fully intend to try and get all our families out. Once we're done in France, we'll head back to base and round up all the families we can, and who wants to come with us."

"But why?" asked Evans.

"Because they are counting on us for safety, and we're not giving it to them. The World is in tatters. Let's be sure to protect what we have."

"Britain isn't lost, is it, Sir?" asked Lewis.

Jones shook his head.

"We're going into France because the country is on its knees, but if Britain is still in the fight, I say let 'em stay."

Jones turned back to Taylor who seemed shocked by the response.

"Can't force them," he said to the Colonel.

It certainly made their lives a little easier, as the logistical nightmare was already giving him a headache even before he considered the risks involved of such an operation.

"How long till we reach Meaux?" Jones asked Rains.

"About twenty minutes, providing we don't hit any more trouble. I'll be hugging the coastline as long as I can."

A flash lit up the cockpit. "Holy shit!" Rains swore loudly.

Jones and Taylor rushed to his side. He was looking down at a battle raging below to the south.

"Guess there is some fight left in France, after all."

Rains banked a little for them to get a better view. For several kilometres, they could see burning wrecks of vehicles from both sides and trench works where troops still fought on, although there seemed little clarity as to where the lines were. It looked more like small skirmishes scattered about the remnants of the epic battle that had been fought there so recently.

"Poor bastards," whispered Jones.

"Same all over, nothing we can do for 'em," replied Taylor.

They carried on silently for their target and awaited some news from Rains.

"That's it!" he finally yelled, "We're on the final stretch to Meaux."

"How does it look?"

"Like a mess, Jones."

He was studying his scanners, but the readings were still being jammed.

"There's a battle going on there, for sure. You want me to put down?"

"No, you let us out and find somewhere safe to wait."

"Safe? You're kidding, right? But you'll have no way to contact me," he replied, looking across at a map on a screen beside them, "I'll put down here," he indicated at a small opening between trees several kilometres north of the base, "If I have to bug out at any point, I'll be airborne and looking for you."

"Not exactly a well structured plan."

"Was any of this?" Taylor asked.

As they flew in towards the base, they could already see Mechs advancing from the west. They had occupied more than a quarter of the base while skirmishes went on throughout many other areas.

"You'll be jumping into a shitstorm," said Rains.

"What's new?" Taylor replied.

"All right, get us over the main walls and let us out there. We'll go the rest of the way on foot."

"You sure?"

"You don't want to get in this fight. We need you and this bird in one piece."

"Yeah, well I'll try to keep her that way. But it seems every time I take Taylor somewhere, he gets us blown to hell."

Taylor and Jones stepped back towards the others and opened the door as they came in. Wind gushed into the crew compartment as they all got to their feet.

"We stay together throughout, and keep it tight!" Jones gave the order.

Rains lifted the nose and put power down on the landing thrusters to bring them to an abrupt halt so that they could jump together. Jones didn't say a word. He simply took a leap out of the door, and the others soon followed. As Taylor hit the ground, he immediately looked back at the copter. Rains got off safely, quickly soaring away, and hugging the ground at the same height he had dropped them off at.

Then he turned his attention to their surroundings. They had landed amongst a number of shipping crates, and they could hear a lot of shouting around them. They lifted their rifles and raised shields in a circle. They could tell they had incoming and had nowhere to go.

A dozen troops rushed into the grouping of containers but did not fire. One was shouting, "Identify yourselves!" in a thick French accent.

Jones immediately lowered his shield and rifle and stepped out in full view, without any concern, and Taylor felt compelled to do the same. The man who had been screaming at them seemed even more surprised to recognise them than he was by their sudden appearance.

"What the hell are you doing here?" he asked, turning to his troops and ordering their weapons down. Their group relaxed and took relief in finding friendly forces.

"Captain Charlie Jones, and this is Colonel Mitch Taylor, Inter..."

"I know who you are," replied the Sergeant excitedly, "We need all the help we can get. You couldn't have come at a better time."

Jones looked to Taylor. He felt for the troops who

looked like they were going through hell. He tried to think of a way of explaining it.

"Where is the rest of your unit?"

"This is it," replied Jones.

The Sergeant turned to Taylor for answers, but Taylor was already giving them before he could open his mouth to ask them.

"France is falling. You must see that. We're here to get one of our own out, and then we're out of here. You should do the same."

The Sergeant was shocked.

"I'm sorry, but we have a mission to accomplish, and we must get on," stated Jones.

With that, he strode forward and in between the Frenchmen, who were left stunned and bewildered. Taylor felt sick to be leaving them to fend for themselves. He didn't recognise a single one of them, but he'd bet good money he'd fought alongside them at one time or another.

"That was cold," he muttered to Jones.

"This is war. We do what we have to do."

Taylor had rarely seen him so determined in all his life, except for after his recovery from the enemy prison camp. His bitter determination had led him to near death then, and it was a warning sign Taylor knew he should take note of, and yet could not find a way to act upon.

Pulses smashed the ground throughout the base, but none came closer than fifty metres to the small group.

They could hear the fiercest fighting was still going on to the east.

"You know that's where we gotta go?" asked Taylor.

Jones nodded as they took a turn and headed right for it.

"Then let's hope the hospital hasn't been overrun," he replied.

"Hope? I got room for a whole lotta hope, but it seems to be what we're living off these days, and it can't carry us through."

"Why? Why can't it?" insisted Jones.

They passed a line of wounded who were being patched up ready to go back into action, and several platoons were going the same direction as them. Nobody even noticed their presence or identity, for they looked no different than any other soldier there.

"Vive la France! Vive la France!" a voice called out.

They looked over at an officer doing his utmost to spur the troops on as he led them forward to join the fight. He was portly for a field officer, and old too. Then they realised it was Dupont, fully armoured and equipped and with rifle in hand. It was the most substantial sign of the times.

"Oh, shit, things must be bad," said Taylor.

Jones ignored it and carried on, but Taylor was right. They both knew that when a General was forced to take up arms at the frontline, it was the beginning of the end.

"There it is!" Taylor shouted.

Jones said nothing as he continued onwards in his laconic determined fashion.

We're almost there! Please be there, please be there, and please be alive! Taylor thought.

It was a straight road leading to the hospital that lay to the northern side of the road. They were just a hundred metres from the door when a building to the south side collapsed, and an enemy tank burst out from the wreckage to block the road. Troops scattered as its turret was brought to bear on them.

"Get down!" Taylor screamed.

The others jumped for cover but not Jones. Before he could take another step, Taylor grabbed him, tossing him into an alleyway for cover and leaping after him. A pulse burst where they had stood seconds before, and two French soldiers who had made a break for cover were vaporised.

Jones was sitting up against a wall, and Taylor leapt on him, grabbing the collar of his armour. He smacked his helmet to get his attention, as he seemed to be in some haze of a dream world.

"We're getting her back, but not like this!" yelled Taylor, "I promise you we'll get her back, but not at the cost of any of our lives! I've seen you like this before, and I don't like it. Don't throw your life away because you're too embittered to think straight!"

Taylor smacked his helmet once more.

"I need your head in the game. I need Captain Jones, the soldier in you, not the single minded headstrong fool who would die through his own pig headedness!"

Jones seemed to take note of the comments and was surprised by the verbal assault that no one had ever levelled at him with such vigour.

"Now, on your feet and follow me!"

Taylor hauled him upwards and immediately jumped the wall, landing on a flat roof. They were looking down on the vast armoured vehicle that was still pounding the street below. They knew they had to move quickly. Taylor ran and jumped onto the next rooftop, and then another, before stopping to see a gaping hole in the second floor of the hospital ahead.

"Ah, shit," he said to himself, and he ran and jumped for the hole, hoping for the best. He tumbled in through the hole and barrelled into a hospital bed that was knocked aside before another finally stopped him. The other five tumbled in just as ungraciously as he had. As they got to their feet, they found themselves surrounded by bodies. The explosion that created their entry point had killed every patient in the room, as well as a doctor and several orderlies.

Jones went frantically from one body to another to check none were Coco, and eventually looked back at Taylor in relief.

"Come on, we need to move fast."

Taylor led them out into the corridor where staff ran back and forth still doing their jobs as if it were just another day. They passed the burnt out wrecked room as if it were not there. As one nurse rushed past, Taylor grabbed her arm and stopped her dead in her tracks. She opened her mouth to complain, but on seeing his rank and grizzled state, held her tongue.

"We're looking for a Sergeant Coco Dubois."

"I'll, I'll have to check the records."

Taylor released his grip and allowed her to lead the way.

She stepped up to a console on the wall and tapped a few buttons before turning back to them.

"I'm sorry, but she's been checked out."

"By who?" Jones demanded.

Taylor half expected it to be Dubois herself, ever persistent to join the fight.

If only that were the case, he thought, as the nurse continued.

"It says she was checked out just a few moments ago under the supervision of Major Martin."

"Martin?" Jones queried.

Taylor thought on it for a moment and began shaking his head.

"If it's the same Martin, he's one of them, a clone!"

Jones face turned to horror, and he rushed through the ward with the others chasing him. He was heading for the

166

nearest outlook over the frontage of the building; Taylor only two paces behind him. They rushed into a busy ward, stopping when they reached a window looking out onto the road. They spotted Coco immediately. She was walking on her own feet and being pushed along by a couple of humans dressed as French officers. Mechs surrounded them as they approached a small transport craft that had put down between several armoured vehicles.

"They're taking her, no!" he screamed at the top of his voice.

Jones reversed his rifle and smashed the window out with it. He put his foot on the edge to climb out, but Taylor got a hold and pulled him back. Jones turned and shoved Taylor back and tried again. Taylor was just as quick and hauled him inside once again. But as he was pushed back as before, he was backed against a wall and found Jones' rifle forced against his chin.

"Don't you stop me!" he cried.

Taylor kept a firm grip on Jones and would not let him move.

"You can save her. We can save her, but not now. We've lost this battle, but not the war. I will not let you die needlessly!"

Jones looked back to the window, and he could see the ship lift off and soar into the distance. He lowered his rifle.

"I've lost her," he said soulfully.

His shoulders were hunched, and he had the look of a defeated man.

"No," replied Taylor, "She's alive, and so are we. We'll find a way. Whatever we have to do, we'll do it. We'll get her back."

CHAPTER EIGHT

Jones sat on the floor, looking helpless. The others fired from positions at the window ledges onto the Mechs below.

"Jones, come on!" Taylor ordered.

Patients were being wheeled out by orderlies, and occasional pulses raced through the room. They kept their heads down. Taylor ducked down to put a fresh magazine in, but as he jumped back to his position, he could see the turret of the tank turn and begin elevating towards them. He quickly looked back to the others.

"Run!" he shouted.

He rushed towards Jones and grabbed him, dragging him towards the archway leading to the corridor. A few seconds later, the room flashed with a blinding light, and they were thrown forwards. Taylor plummeted right through an interior wall that did little to slow him down.

As the dust began to settle, he got to his feet. All of them had made it, but the room they had been in was devastated. The floor had collapsed onto people below, and part of the ceiling was also missing. They could see right out to the enemy positions and soon rushed to cover.

"What are we gonna do?" asked Robinson.

Taylor paused to think for a moment; there seemed to be no easy answer. He looked down at Jones, who still seemed oblivious to the danger around them. He looked up and asked.

"Why did they take her?"

Taylor hadn't had any time to think about it, but now his head was filled with sinister thoughts he'd rather not have there.

"A whole hospital full of patients, a base full of soldiers, why her, Mitch?" Jones continued.

"I doubt it is any coincidence," replied Taylor.

"How do you mean, Sir?" Lewis asked.

"You all know this Erdogan guy, whatever he is, wants to bring me down. It's not just about me. It's about us. It's about what our unit stands for, and what we're famed for. He wants to make us suffer for his own amusement and for all to see."

"A whole world war, and he wants a piece of us that badly?" Wood asked.

"It's not as crazy as it sounds," Jones joined in, "It's starting to make a little sense."

"I wouldn't be surprised if she was taken to try and draw us into some trap. Maybe they expected to find us here? But they can't know we're here yet. I bet you a tonne of credits, they were hoping this would draw us out," said Taylor.

Jones shook his head. "I dunno, but I don't like it. Obviously, the fact they have taken her, but the whole thing stinks."

"Yes it does, but we've come back from worse," replied Taylor, "Right now, there is nothing we can do for Dubois but survive and keep up the fight, so that is what I need you all to do. A distracted man is a dead man, got it?"

Jones nodded, although it was clear he wouldn't be able to isolate the thoughts which plagued him, and Taylor knew he wouldn't be able to either.

"Someone's gotta take out that tank," said Robinson.

"You volunteering?" Taylor asked.

"With what?"

"Yeah, exactly."

"They could hear the pounding of footsteps coming up the fire escape stairs at the end of the hallway just a few metres beside them. They turned and readied their weapons, as now they weren't even sure which humans were on their side. Dupont rushed out onto the floor and stopped on seeing the Colonel.

"Taylor? What in the hell are you doing back here?"

"Good to see you, too, Sir. We came for Captain Jones'

171

wife."

"Well, what are you still doing here?" he asked, pacing up to Taylor.

"Well, she's gone," he replied.

The General turned to Jones. "My condolences, Captain."

"No, Sir, she's not dead. She was just taken by the enemy. Spirited away on one of their craft. They sent clones in here to take her away."

Dupont was perplexed by the idea, but he was a lot more open minded about such things after everything he had experienced.

"So she was taken alive?"

Jones nodded. Dupont shook his head. "Then my condolences still, for I would not wish capture on anyone, anymore than I would death. This is a cruel and horrifying enemy."

"Which is why it is imperative we get her back as soon as we can," replied Taylor.

Another shell hit the building further along, and they felt the floor tremble beneath them.

"We gotta do something about that tank," said Taylor.

"We?" asked Dupont. He carried on past them with several French soldiers, carrying what had been come to know as RAT launchers - Reitech Anti-tank Launchers.

"Can't touch that damn thing from the front, and we can't get around it with Mechs crawling all over the place."

"You think it'll be weak on top, like our armour?"

"You better hope so," he replied.

Taylor followed them to the gaping hole they had recently fled from.

"Fire when ready," ordered Dupont.

Four RAT carriers took a knee and readied their weapons. The first fired without hesitation and saw it strike a corner of the turret and soar off into the ground before exploding. They saw bright light sparks ignite from the impact.

"What the hell do they put in those things?"

"God knows, Robinson," Taylor sighed.

The other gunners looked weary now and took their time.

"Come on, damn you, shoot," Dupont ordered.

The second fired and hit the top turret, causing an immense explosion that they had to look away from. But as they looked back, they could see it had put a dent in the armour and chipped away a little, but nothing of note. Then they noticed the turret pivoting their way.

"Oh, that's not good," Taylor grimaced.

"Don't aim for the turret. Shoot in front of it, down into the upper hull!" Jones hollered.

The gunners looked to Dupont for confirmation.

"Go on, do it!" he shouted as the barrel came in line to their position. The two of them fired almost simultaneously and landed the shots in front of the turret, almost in the exact same spot. The first ignited on the surface, and the second went right through the impact. An explosion ripped through the vehicle, as two hatches were blown open and smoke belched from them.

A cheer rang out from the troops on the ground, but not from those in the hospital. Dupont sighed in relief. He was as surprised they were still alive as Taylor was. But in the distance they could see more vehicles approaching, and Mechs still sweeping towards them. Hospital beds continued to be wheeled past them and walking wounded were being helped to the stairs.

"We have to get the wounded out of here," Taylor said.

"You keep talking about this 'we', Colonel, but you didn't come here to fight alongside us."

"No, Sir, but we're here now, and that's just the way it is. So let's get them out to somewhere safe."

"And where would that be? Krys forces have all but surrounded us, and are taking this base one block at a time."

They looked down. The Mechs were encircling the hospital even as they spoke.

"I doubt you could get out now, even if you wanted to."

"Then have them fight. Every one of them capable of lifting and firing a rifle, have them do so."

Dupont thought about it for a moment, and he knew it was a desperate measure.

"They'll only die if we fail here anyway, so let them at

least have a hand in deciding their own fate."

Dupont gritted his teeth and rubbed his chin, finally nodding in agreement. He looked over to one of his own soldiers.

"Do it."

He looked back to Taylor. "You should know that Washington has fallen, so to has New York, Baltimore, and many more. Obliterated."

"I was at Baltimore."

"Then I am sorry, Colonel."

Taylor didn't know so many had been destroyed, but it didn't surprise him at all after what he had seen and experienced.

"You're stuck here, you know that, right?"

Taylor nodded. "I've been stuck in many places in my life, General, and yet here I stand today, unstuck from all of them."

"That's right. The shit just seems to slide right off you," he replied, trying to smile.

They looked down to see the gunfire in the street below was already intensifying. The Mechs drove onwards past the burning wreck of the knocked out tank.

"Where do you want me, General?"

"Wherever you can do the most damage."

With that, he carried on towards the far eastern side of the building and took up position in a corner ward that had already been fully evacuated. Part of wall was missing, and that provided an excellent loophole for the few men he had to use. Taylor pulled out several magazines from his webbing. He lay down prone and put them in front of him as he looked out onto the base below.

"You taking up residency, Sir?"

"Looks that way, Robinson."

Jones lay down beside him and did the same. It was the first sign that he had heeded Taylor's words, and he nodded in gratitude for it.

"I need you, Charlie, and you know it. We stick together, see each other through, then we'll get her back."

Jones looked out of the hole and could see a number of Mechs advancing towards them without any attempt to use cover. They didn't need to, as nobody was putting up resistance.

"You better hope Dupont has some ammunition on tap because we're gonna need it."

"Yep," Taylor said casually.

He took aim with his rifle dead centre on the head of the first creature he set eyes on. He squeezed the trigger, and the well-aimed shot went clean through and dropped the Mech warrior instantly.

"That's how it's done," said Taylor.

The others took up positions either side him as if it were a shooting gallery and joined in. A shot rang out every two seconds from that hole as each of them took careful shots. By the time the first five Mechs had fallen, the rest were starting to take cover and respect the danger posed to them.

"You think we'll get out of this?" Jones whispered.

"Of course we will. We always do."

Jones wasn't sure if he were joking or had such unwavering confidence, but it amused him either way. It was the first smile Taylor had seen on Jones face since they got there.

"That doesn't look good," said Wood.

They looked back. The enemy numbers were growing, and armoured vehicles backed up by air support were behind them. Taylor quickly took aim at the first target he could and opened fire, and did not stop until every magazine laid out before him was empty. He got to one knee and felt around his webbing to find he had just a single magazine left. He looked down to Jones who had just found the same. As Mitch put the last of his ammunition into his rifle, he lay back down and took aim once more.

Mech bodies lay strewn about, although more still advanced, and many with shields now, too. He took in a breath and held it. He was about to squeeze the trigger when an explosion struck a group of Mechs in front of them. He looked away from his sight, and another four landed all around the first.

"Those aren't Krys shells. They're ours," said Jones.

Taylor stood up so he could look from what was left of the window. In the distance, he could see constant muzzles flashes and could just make out the silhouettes of French tanks approaching from the north and firing on the move.

"Holy shit," was all he could think to say.

"Where on Earth did they come from?"

"Guess the fight ain't quite over yet, Charlie."

They could hear cheering from the streets and watched as many of the enemy vehicles and armour turned to face them. As they did, another artillery barrage smashed the positions in front of them, and a wing of friendly fighters soared in towards the Mech craft.

"You see, Colonel; France is not finished yet."

Taylor looked around; Dupont stood in the archway behind them. He looked back to see the Mechs were already retreating towards the armour, and he knew they had gained a respite.

"Sir, I must appeal to you for help," said Jones.

He looked back to Taylor who nodded in agreement.

"My resources are pretty thin, but I will do what I can for you, Captain."

"My wife. She was here as I said, taken from here by Krys agents or collaborators, or whatever."

"Yes, and I am deeply sorry for that."

"I don't need sympathy, Sir. I need her back, and I'll do whatever I have to for that to happen."

"I don't know what I can do to help, Captain."

"You have resources. You can use them to find out where that ship went, and where she has been taken."

"It's a pretty long shot," he replied, turning to leave.

Jones grabbed his arm and stopped him.

"I'll take any kind of shot," he replied, knowing it had multiple meanings and was not lost on the General. Dupont turned back fully and thought about it for a moment.

"If I could do this, and I say if, it would take an immense amount of non-frontline staff to pursue it. Resources that are vitally needed elsewhere. What would you be willing to do for me?"

"You're holding me to ransom over finding my wife?" he pleaded.

He looked to Taylor for support, but he didn't get any.

"Tough times," Taylor said, "Take what you can get."

"What is it you want, General?"

Dupont looked over to Taylor.

"I want you. You've accomplished some incredible things against this enemy. I have reports of Erdogan's position. I suggested nuking the bastard, but apparently, his defence systems would stop anything we throw at him. And then there is you."

Taylor could already see where this was going. He always knew he would have to face the alien leader, but he never for a moment thought it could be so soon.

"Oh, no, no, you don't. You want me to go get my head blown off on some crazy ass mission..."

He stopped, noticing Jones pleading eyes; they were

hard to ignore.

"Why not?" Jones asked him, "You've beaten these bastards before. You could end it all now."

"Yeah, or probably die and be a martyr without a following alive to remember."

He turned away and looked out to the tank battle raging in the distance. He shook his head, thinking of the fear he had felt at the prospect of facing Erdogan. Finally, he turned back and asked, "Where is he?"

"Munich."

"He's here? On Earth?" Taylor asked in surprise.

"All the reports I have would say yes, but there's nothing I can do about it. I can't spare anything, and even if I could, it would never work. But you and your particular set of skills, you have a chance."

Taylor looked to Jones who was only waiting for him to say yes.

"I'll think about it."

"Well think fast. Time is not on our side, Colonel."

"What is to think about, Mitch?"

"This is not a decision to be made lightly, Jones."

"Every moment we delay the search for Coco, we reduce our chances of finding her."

Taylor nodded in agreement.

"Fifteen minutes is all I ask."

Dupont agreed and left the room. The six remaining gathered into a circle, as they had all heard the facts. They waited for Taylor to speak, and after some consideration, he did.

"Going after Erdogan will be like nothing we have ever done before. He's smarter and stronger than anything we've ever dealt with. I honestly believe it will cost the lives of whoever goes, whether they succeed or not."

They were stunned and speechless by his assessment. They had never heard Taylor speak in such a defeatist manner. He walked over to the window and looked out across the battlefield beyond. Friendly armour continued to advance, and it was a welcome sight to see their forces making progress, but he knew it would be a rare sight. Jones paced up beside him and looked out at the same scene.

"You have a chance to end this," he said.

"An opportunity, but I'm not so sure I've got a chance."

"Of course you have a chance."

"No, you stop. You'll say whatever you need to here; whatever is necessary for you to get what you want."

Jones turned face on to Taylor.

"No. I would never have you sacrifice yourself. Why can't there be multiple reasons for my actions? I want Coco to be safe, of course, but she never will be while Erdogan is alive."

"What'll it be, Colonel?"

Taylor looked around. Dupont was in the room once more. It was nowhere near the time he had asked for, but he could see the urgency in the General's face.

"Let's do it," he replied.

"Then follow me."

Taylor knew he had so few options left, and at least this way, he had a shot at doing some good. Dupont led them out of the hospital and back through the base. Outside at a bunker they were heading towards, they could see a copter and Rains waiting beside it.

"What happened to staying put?" Taylor asked him as they approached.

"Things were looking up, and I figured you'd need me here."

"Looking up?" asked Taylor, somewhat confused.

Dupont led them into a bunker and into his war room. Every single one of the personnel inside was fully combat equipped, a sign of the desperate times.

"So what have you got on Erdogan?" Taylor asked.

"What I already told you."

"Wait, what? You know a city, and that's it?"

Dupont shrugged.

"No, no, no. If I'm gonna do this, I need intel. I need a location. I need enemy positions, surveillance of the locations. Come on, I need something!"

He looked to Jones for support.

"Please, Mitch, just go with it."

Taylor nodded.

"Captain, I'll give you three of my best people to help

you track down your wife. I have absolute confidence in them, and I assure you they will do everything in their power," said Dupont, as he pointed and ushered Jones over to a corner of the room.

Jones looked back as he went there. He felt guilty to be leaving his best friend, but he could not stop his search for Coco. As he reached the desk, he could see a surveillance video shot from the hospital with a still of Coco being led to the craft she had left on. It immediately grabbed his attention, and he couldn't look away.

"That's her," he said.

The young female officer at the desk before him looked eager to assist.

"We're tracking the flight path of the craft at the moment, Captain, but with most of the satellites down and our connections to what's left, it's proving difficult. I am Lieutenant Bisset, and I will do everything I can to help, along with my colleagues, Sir."

Taylor ignored her introduction and delved right into the facts.

"Where did the ship come from?"

"Well, that's a little easier," replied the woman, "We can first identify it coming out of northern Germany. It was unarmed and alone, and therefore not considered hostile."

"But it came from enemy territory?"

"Yes, Sir, but frankly, it's a mess out there. Civilian craft are coming and going, and nobody is attempting to stop them. Refugees are pouring over borders, and deserters too."

"What else have you got?"

"We're still pursuing all leads. I believe we can pinpoint their final destination with relative accuracy within a few hours. We could do with a few more eyes to go over the information we have."

"I'll do whatever I can, just find her."

He looked over to Taylor and nodded as a sign of gratitude. Taylor looked back to Dupont.

"So Erdogan is in Munich, what other information or resources can you give me?"

"Honestly, nothing. I've given what help I can to your Captain, and I have told you where you can find the alien leader. We'll keep on fighting them on every front we can. Now it's up to you to strike at the heart of the enemy. And with that, I must leave you. I have a lot to do and little time to do it. Good luck, Colonel."

Dupont turned to some of his command staff and left Taylor to his own devices. Taylor shook his head and wondered what the hell was happening. He stepped outside for some fresh air and to think if it wasn't all just a dream. He was greeted first by Rains with a big smile on his face.

"So what's the plan, boss?" he asked.

"Singlehandedly bring the about the destruction of the enemy leader."

Rains laughed.

"Of course, because anything lesser would be beneath you," he joked.

He stopped smiling on seeing Taylor's deadly serious expression.

"No, you can't be serious?"

"Sadly, yes. We've got a shot, but I've got no idea how we'll pull it off."

"And Jones, where is he?"

"On his own mission. We'll have to go without him. Evans, Wood, you're with Jones. Do whatever you can to help. The rest of you are with me."

"So it's what, the four of us? I know we've pulled off some pretty impressive shit over the years, but don't you think you're being a little overly ambitious with this?"

Taylor nodded in agreement.

"Aren't we always? Let's not look for problems. Let's look for solutions."

He led them around a corner to where empty ammunition crates had been stacked and took a seat on one while the others joined him.

"What's our time frame?" Rains asked.

"No idea, but we have to do this ASAP."

"And how do you intend to kill him?"

Taylor shrugged. "Working on a few ideas."

"I hate to say it, but we need help."

Taylor stopped, looking up into the sky as he mulled it

over in his head. He knew his situation was an impossible one, and he couldn't find a sensible answer to their problems.

"So what do we do?"

"First thing is we gotta get into Germany, Eddie. They may have got across the border unnoticed or contested, but I doubt we'll be so lucky. Neither can we go in by force."

"So what options are left?"

"We go in as civilians."

"As spies you mean? Minute we take off our uniforms and go into hostile territory, we aren't marines anymore; we aren't soldiers. We aren't enemy combatants. We are clandestine forces and will be shot as spies."

"Are you serious? All the danger we've gone through, and your biggest concern is being shot? We could have been shot and killed any time today, yesterday, and any one of hundreds of days in the war."

"But we'd do it in our colours, as who we are."

Taylor was surprised it meant so much to him. For a man who flaunted all the rules of uniform, the prospect of going without his identity scared him.

"I need you," replied Taylor.

"Damn right you do," he replied in a quivering tone, "Cos I'm the only son of a bitch stupid enough to do what you ask."

Taylor smiled in response and got up to pat him on the

shoulder.

"That's right, but you've got us all this far, haven't you?"

Taylor took in a deep breath. Some ideas were finally coming to him, and he knew he had to at least give them a shot.

"Eddie, your job is to find us transport. Something small and civilian that won't draw any attention."

"Round here?"

"I didn't say it would be easy. Just get it done."

He turned to the other two.

"Next, you will find us clothing. We need to look convincing as civilians, so find us the appropriate stuff."

"Where, Sir?" Lewis asked.

"Gentlemen, this is a country ravaged by war where civilians are fleeing for their lives. Finding some clothes shouldn't be an issue. Go to the nearest highway, and I bet you good money, you'll find it backed up with cars packed with clothing from those without the cash to fly out of the warzone. So go and forage for whatever you can get."

"You want us to pillage from what refugees have left on the road?" Robinson asked in disgust.

"Let's get this straight," Taylor spoke sternly, "These are desperate times. You've seen it for yourself; so we don't have time to get all soft and mushy over things we can neither affect nor help with in any way, other than by what we are already doing. Let's focus on winning this war. It's what we have a right and duty to do, no matter what, you got it?"

None of them liked it, but they accepted it.

"So if we get transport and clothes, we might get close to Munich, but then what? It's not like we can just walk in and put a bullet in Erdogan's head. How are we gonna get close to him, and even then, how are we gonna kill him?" Rains asked.

"There are plenty of humans working with the enemy. We should be able to blend in fine. How we get that close to Erdogan, well I dunno, but we'll figure something out. And how we kill him? You've got me. We'll figure much of this out as we go along."

"You know this is a complete fucking disaster waiting to happen?"

Taylor nodded. "Isn't everywhere around us in as bad a state? What else would you have me do?"

"Get some help. Find some support to get us through this. Otherwise, we're just throwing our lives away because we can't think of anything else. You've got this far because you've had others to rely on and see you through. We're here for you, but we aren't enough."

Taylor knew it was true. His friends had kept him winning all along. He tried to think of how he could gain some support, but he was running out of friends to turn to. He looked to the other two.

"Rains has had a whole lot to say, what do you think?"

They were surprised and speechless. Clearly, they were

not used to officers asking them their opinion.

"Well, come on, speak your mind."

"Sir…" replied Robinson, "we need help. We need manpower, we need weapons, and we need the resources to make this mission happen, or we're just pissing in the wind."

Taylor nodded in agreement. "Then you have my word. I'll get us the support we need."

CHAPTER NINE

Taylor rushed back into Dupont's bunker.

"I need to talk to General Heath in Pittsburgh. You can make that happen, can't you?" he demanded.

"Probably, but I don't know what good it will do you, Colonel."

"You let me worry about that. You haven't got the resources to give me, fine. But you need to help me get them elsewhere."

Dupont turned to his comms officer and nodded in agreement to carry out Taylor's request. They stood waiting for several minutes before they finally got a response from Pittsburgh.

"I'm sorry, but General Heath is not available at this time," a voice replied.

"Taylor rushed across the room, stopped the comms operator from speaking, and did so himself.

"This Colonel Mitch Taylor. Get the General on the line immediately," he commanded.

The line went quiet, and they waited for thirty seconds before a response finally came through.

"Taylor, where the hell are you?" Heath asked.

"Sir, I'm here with General Dupont in Northern France, but that doesn't matter. What matters is we have an opportunity to..."

"Opportunity!" screamed Heath, "Goddamn it, Taylor, you left your post and left this fight! Get your ass back here now!"

"Can't do that, Sir. What I'm doing here is too important."

"I'll tell you what is important, Colonel, the survival of the United States and its people. We need every goddamn fighting man and woman in this country on side and with a rifle in hand. You need to get some perspective here."

"Yes, Sir, perspective is exactly what I have. If I can have just a few moments of your time."

Heath gave a long and drawn out sigh and finally answered, "You've got one minute to explain yourself, and if I'm not convinced, I want you on a ship back here, got it?"

Taylor ignored the question because he could not rightfully accept the deal when he knew he might well have to break it.

"Sir, we have a chance to end this with one precision

strike."

"What are you talking about?"

Taylor turned to Dupont. "Is this line definitely secure? I mean, beyond all doubt."

Dupont nodded, and Taylor had to gamble on the fact he was right.

"Sir, I know where Erdogan is. I want to take a shot at taking him out, but I need help."

"That it?" Heath asked.

Taylor looked to Dupont and shrugged in surprise.

"I have no time for your wild ideas, Taylor. We've got a war on our hands, like nothing we've ever seen before. We need you. Your people need you. Get back here and do your duty."

"Negative, Sir. I will do my duty, but if that conflicts with your orders, then so be it."

"You will obey my command, Colonel."

"No, Sir, I won't. I fought alongside you because our paths coincided, but I am not under your command."

"You can't just pick and choose which orders you follow, Colonel. You are an officer in the United States Marine Corps!"

Taylor hit the end transmission button, and it instantly cut off before the General could condemn him further.

"Any other day, I'd say you should follow the orders of your command chain. But now I know why you do what you do. Your passion burns deep, and you always do what you believe is best. You're not always right, but I respect your motivation," Dupont said.

"Thanks, I guess," he replied.

"I am under no illusions that the mission I am asking you to undertake is a suicidal one, but you need to know I have no agenda in doing so, except what we all share; a will to win and survive as a species. I wish you every luck, Taylor, and I have every confidence in you."

Taylor looked over at Jones. He still had his head buried in a screen and had been oblivious to his presence and discussion throughout. He knew his friend was useless to him while the chance of getting Dubois back remained a possibility.

* * *

Two hours later Taylor stood before a small civilian craft as Rains made a few last patches to it. He stood in a simple pair of cargo trousers and leather jacket now. The only weapon he carried was his sidearm, and that was concealed in a shoulder holster he had acquired from Dupont's stores. The others had done likewise, though Rains had the smallest changes to make to blend in as a civilian.

"Stow all our armour and weapons aboard. We will surely need them," he said to Lewis.

"We're really flying into enemy territory like this, in that thing?" Robinson asked.

"Hey!" Rains shouted, "She's my girl, and I won't hear a word against her!"

"Where did you even find her?"

"She was one of the base officer's personal transports until she was laid up last year. She's done some distance. Well run in."

It was a small copter, just large enough for eight people and a little cargo. Its dark navy paintwork had faded from years in the sun, and it displayed no markings of any kind.

"She really flies?" Taylor asked.

"Oh, sure. By all accounts she's solid. She just got replaced by a newer model, from what I hear."

"She looks twenty years old," Lewis joked.

"Twenty-two, I believe," replied Eddie, as he turned to face Lewis and smiled.

"You think this is a good idea, Sir?"

"I can't see a problem with her, Robinson. Looks solid to me."

"I meant overall, Sir. I wouldn't mind crossing the Channel in this bird, but going into enemy territory. She has no weapon systems, no counter-measures, no armour, and she can probably be outrun by everything out there."

"But she'll get us there," Eddie added.

"Yeah, we aren't blundering through the border, Corporal. We're slipping past unnoticed. Can you think of a better ship to do that in?"

"We're about good to go," stated Rains.

They climbed aboard, but none of them could quite believe they were really going ahead with it.

"I hope you've got a good plan, Sir."

"I've got a plan for sure, Robinson, but how good it is only time will tell."

Taylor hit the door button, but nothing happened at all.

"Yeah...the uh, hydraulics are out on a few non-essential items!" Eddie called from his cockpit.

"Good start," muttered Taylor, as he grabbed the door and wrenched it shut. He slid down the manual door lock and sat down with the other two. It was such a small craft; he was just half a metre behind the pilot's chair when he took a seat.

As they lifted off, Eddie looked back and asked, "All right, it's just us now, so what's the plan?"

"We need manpower and support. We can't get it from our side, so we'll have to get it inside Germany."

Rains shook his head. "You ain't got no friends over there no more, have you?"

"That's where you're wrong Rains. After the Moon was finally abandoned, the US donated the remains of the Ramstein base as a new home for them."

"You're kidding, right?"

"No, why would I?"

"Okay, so you reckon Kelly will help?"

"He'd better. He owes us both, big time."

Rains turned back to the controls and had them on their

way in no time. It took them just thirty minutes to reach the border. They could see lines of military vehicles, both alien and UEN, but more than anything were civilians.

"Look at them, passing the enemy by as if it's just another day."

Taylor got up to stand beside Rains and look out for himself.

"What else would you have them do? Not like they can fight back."

Most of the civilian movement was heading into Germany.

"But the Krys, they are letting them live?"

"Yes, Erdogan is keeping us fighting each other. He realised we are too strong when unified. He's probably promised the UEN leaders everything under the sun."

"None of which he will deliver."

Taylor nodded in agreement.

"I can't believe they are falling for that shit. Have they forgotten the wars we fought across these countries so recently?"

"Most people don't want to remember. They just want to be left to live in peace. They're only siding with whoever they think will bring an end to their suffering."

"And what do you think, Sir? Should we keep on fighting?" Robinson asked yet another question.

He turned around to see the other two peering over his shoulder.

"Damn right we should. Day we give up is the end of us all. The moment Erdogan can seize power globally, he would have us killed in our sleep."

"You sure?" Lewis asked.

"Yeah, I'm sure," he snapped.

"And if we kill this Erdogan, you think it would bring an end to the fighting, Sir?"

Taylor shook his head. "No, Lewis, but I think it would be a start."

"A start?" asked Robinson, "We've been fighting these wars for years, have we not even achieved a start yet?"

Taylor looked at them and could see the desperation in their faces.

"We won those wars and won them well, don't you forget it. This is a new war, and what we did before it counts for shit if we can't win this one."

"We're about half a klick from the border now," Rains interrupted him.

Taylor turned his attention to the view ahead of them. They could see anti-aircraft emplacements on the ground, and a number of UEN ships patrolling the border above them.

"You better hope they don't know who we are now, as running ain't an option," Eddie added.

"We'll be fine."

"Yeah, why's that?"

"Because we always are, because we've done everything

right, and because it's our destiny."

"Destiny? Holy shit I never took you for a religious man."

"I'm not. But we both know, when all is said and done, I have to face Erdogan. It will happen. It has to happen."

"And that helps us here, because?"

"Because this isn't our end, not even close. We have too much left to do."

Rains shook his head at the logic.

"Here it is."

He held his breath as they cruised on over the border amongst a line of other ships of all sizes.

"They don't even seem to care," said Eddie.

"Why would they? What have they got to worry about?" Robinson asked.

"Yeah, Mechs are doing the fighting for them. As far as they're concerned, they can just sit back with the popcorn and enjoy the show," replied Taylor.

"If a little light genocide is your kind of thing, yeah," joked Rains.

Taylor smiled just a little until he realised how sad but true Rains was. A UEN fighter suddenly soared into view and matched their speed to inspect them visually. Taylor quickly ducked back from the cockpit.

"This ain't good, Eddie," he said, as he sat back down and hoped.

"Take it easy. It's just a fly by."

Taylor could feel the sweat dripping down his face. A shame after he'd washed off the dirt and grime before changing into civilian attire, but he knew he wouldn't stay clean for long.

"What are they doing?" he asked.

"Just checking us out. Seeing if I look legit."

"Legit what?"

He looked over to the pilot in the fighter who was just fifteen metres beside them and smiled.

"Checking out if I'm a civi or not."

Rains gave him the thumbs up and waved to play the fool.

"I don't think you were ever at risk of looking like you have ever worn a uniform."

"I'll take that as a compliment."

He went silent as they continued on their path and hoped.

"You know how hot it is in here? Goddamn sauna," Taylor complained.

"Yeah, can't say the compressors work too well. We got air, but that's about it."

"You really did find a piece of junk this time."

An uncomfortable silence crept in once more, and Taylor could see even Rains was starting to worry a little.

This is going on too long, Taylor thought.

"If he tries to contact us, you ignore him, you hear? Pretend our comms unit is down."

"Well, it is," replied Eddie.

Taylor grimaced. "That figures."

"What's wrong with talking to them?" Robinson asked.

"Two Brits and two Americans trying to cross over the border into Germany, the key member of the UEN, how d'you think that would go down?" responded Taylor.

"It's okay. He's moving on!" Eddie yelled jubilantly.

Taylor signed in relief.

"All right, then you know where to go. Keep a steady pace, and don't draw any more attention than we need to."

"How many men does Kelly have, Sir?"

"Not entirely sure, Robinson."

"And their loyalties?"

Taylor shook his head. "Officially, Ramstein was still US soil, despite it being allocated to the Moon colonists, but I can guarantee it will have been annexed by Germany early on in this war."

"So, who knows what state we'll find them in?"

"Kelly is our only hope now, so I'm willing to take that chance."

The sun was going down, a fact Taylor was glad of as they approached Ramstein.

"That's it," Rains said, pointing to a set of landing lights and marked landing zones. The lights of a main street were also lit up, as well as several other residential roads nearby. "What do you want me to do?"

"Put down as if it were any other day. We aren't trying

to hide anything."

"Aside from our weapons, our intentions, or our mission?" he asked.

"Just do it."

"They're not even in blackout, Sir," Robinson said.

"Why would they be? They've got nothing to fear."

The area was quiet, and they could see no sign of a military presence. Rains brought the copter down to a perfect and smooth landing.

"What now?"

"We roll into town. We're just civilian refugees from France who aren't looking for any trouble.

"We don't exactly sound very French," Lewis replied.

"No, we are reporters working out of Paris. At least Eddie looks the part."

"Yeah thanks," he replied.

Taylor once more heaved the door with his own body. He'd gotten so used to living in the Reitech suit that it felt bizarre to have to use so much of his own bodily strength for common actions.

"Going into hostile lands without our gear, without intel, and without backup, I don't like this."

Taylor nodded. "I know, just follow my lead, Robinson."

There was no one there to greet them at the landing port. Fifty metres away, they could see a guard station and a few local officers hanging out inside, but they paid them little attention.

"You see," said Taylor, "We're just a few guys rolling into town."

"Whatever you say, boss."

Taylor led them on towards the main street. Everything around them was new, not a building more than three years old. The structures were simple and mostly concrete. Bright colourful lights scattered about every building made a poor attempt at livening the place up. There was no grass, no trees. It was a concrete hell.

"Hell of a place to live," whispered Lewis.

"Walk in the park after living on the Moon," Rains joined in.

"It's true. Those colonists who established the Lunar colony, and their children after them, are people with simple tastes. They wanted to pioneer a new simpler way of life after all the complexities of Earth. Or that's how Kelly once explained it to me," added Taylor.

"And here they are, slap bang on Earth in the middle of it all," Rains said.

In a hundred metres to the main street, they only saw two people who were on the far side of the road. Taylor put it down to the weather, as it was certainly chilled.

"Got a plan here?"

"Kelly invited me here many times between the wars, Eddie. Every time I was too busy or working, or that's what I told him. Now here I am wishing I had come visiting. Then we'd know where the hell he was. As it is, we'll find the most popular bar in town. I'd bet good money we'll find him there."

"Can't be many bars round here. Population's probably no more than a thousand or two."

The road branched out into a thoroughfare, and groups of teenagers were scattered about drinking and talking amongst themselves. Taylor and the others stopped and could not help but staring. It was as if life was going on like nothing had ever happened. Taylor surveyed the rest of the scene. There were three bars about the centre of the town.

"All right, so which is it?" Rains asked.

"We'll hit the nearest one and work from there."

They strode into an establishment called The Moon Dweller.

"Subtle," muttered Rains.

"More than you are," Taylor grinned.

They stepped in to find it half full, and utterly alien to them. The concrete theme of the street continued into the establishment itself. Even the bar was cast from concrete and part of the structure itself. Stools and tables were made of minimalist metal design, and a lack of decor hardly made for a welcome appearance. The light was fairly low and casting long shadows.

Most patrons turned to face the newcomers with suspicion, all but a pair of soldiers sitting at the bar. It did not go unnoticed by Taylor. It was clear to him the soldiers were not locals, for they could not recognise residents over strangers. A tune played in the background that sounded like artificial electronically created garbage to Taylor, and it made his brain hurt.

"What can I get you?"

Taylor looked to the bar, and a middle-aged man behind it greeted them with a smile, though he did not recognise him.

"I'll take four of whatever you recommend."

"Hey, we ain't got time for this," whispered Rains.

"We don't have a choice. You see those two soldiers over there. Look a little closer. They're UEN."

Rains shot a quick glance over and was shocked he hadn't noticed before.

"Right then, so what do we do?"

"Play it cool, Eddie."

He looked back to the others. You call me John, okay?"

They nodded in agreement as they reached the bar, and the barman began passing over the first two drinks. They were served in tall thin glasses and were a vibrant blood red, almost metallic. A metal stone of some kind sat in the bottom of the glass, and the beverage was warm to the touch.

"Redrock. Invented and brewed by the first of the Moon colonists, and popular ever since," added the barman with a smile. He passed over the other two drinks, and then put a credit chip scanner on the top beside them with their bill. Taylor reached into his pocket to pay but stopped, realising he could not use his name for anything. He looked to Eddie.

"Your time to pay, my friend."

Eddie sighed, and it was not at all put on. He pulled out his card and held it up before the scanner.

"I thank you kindly... Edmund Rains, how do I know that name?"

"Eddie Rains?" a voice called out.

Oh shit, Taylor thought.

They turned around. A man with a smile on his face was approaching. Taylor instantly recognised him as Doyle, one of the MDF soldiers he had fought alongside years earlier. He turned away and tried to hide his face.

"Rains, you're the man who flew food and ammo to us in our darkest days. I never got to meet you in person. You did good by us!"

He reached out his hand and shook it but stopped when he noticed Taylor trying to hide his face behind Lewis. Doyle stopped and had to make a second take. "Taylor?" he whispered. He leaned in closer, "What the hell are you doing here? You can't be here."

Taylor turned and faced the man, knowing he could no longer hide.

"Good to see you, too, Doyle."

"I don't think you understand, Sir..."

Taylor interrupted him before he could continue.

"I get it. I'm in UEN territory. I know. But are you not neutral?"

Doyle shook his head. "MDF signed up with the UEN when all this began, but once the EA broke away, Kelly told them where to stick it, and we've been disbanded."

"So you're being kept prisoner in your own town?"

Doyle nodded. "Pretty much."

"And Kelly?"

"Under house arrest. He caused some trouble early on, and now he's under constant watch."

"I knew it was a waste of time coming here," Rains muttered.

"Excuse me!" an authoritative voice called out in a German accent.

Their conversation immediately halted, and they turned to see the two UEN soldiers standing a few metres away in a clear attempt to confront the newcomers.

"They're with us, old friends," said Doyle.

The man who had spoken was a corporal; he stood tall and proud, with a square jaw and a formidably strong build.

"We'll be the judge of that," he replied, "Let's see your ID cards."

"We're just passing through. We aren't here to cause any trouble."

"ID cards now!" yelled the Corporal.

Taylor could already see there was no chance of talking

their way out of it. He looked around the room at the antipathy and hatred towards the soldiers from most of those in the room. He recognised a few faces, and he could tell as he presented his face to them, many recognised him, too. He smiled, seeing he had the support of the room.

"Well, no problem, Corporal," he replied.

He was deliberately over friendly as to try and have the Corporal relax. He took a few paces closer, drew out his card from his pocket, and handed it to the Corporal. The man pulled out an e-reader from his chest pocket but stopped just before he scanned the card, looking at the name on it. He looked up just in time to see Taylor's fist connect with his nose.

To Taylor's horror the impact barely moved the Corporal's face, and he quickly returned a punch of his own that felt like a freight train. Taylor was knocked back, and he sprawled over against the counter of the bar. He got back up and shook it off.

Damn!

The giant German rushed towards him in an opposing fashion. He stood a good bit taller than Taylor and looked more like a bodybuilder than a soldier. The exact moment he reached Taylor, a bar stool seemed to come out of nowhere in the hands of Robinson. It smashed into the man and broke his nose. He stumbled back unceremoniously. As he did, Lewis jumped towards him, kicked his kneecap out, and then struck down on his collarbone to drive him down further.

Despite the pain, the German got back up and drove a heavy uppercut into Lewis' stomach and another to his face that forced him back towards Taylor. He had now righted himself. The German Corporal reached for his sidearm, and that was all the indication Taylor needed. He ripped his pistol from his holster and fired a quick shot that struck almost dead centre between the man's eyes. The Reitech round went right through and hit a wall the far side of the room.

The man dropped dead like a stone, and Taylor quickly took aim at the second as he reached for his pistol. He stopped and froze.

"Don't even think about it!" Taylor shouted.

Rains was quick to slip past the man and grab his pistol from him. They looked around. At first the crowd in the bar ground didn't appear to know what to think until Doyle finally began to clap and cheer. The rest then joined in. He looked over to the two Brits who had leapt to his aid.

"You boys fight dirty," he told them.

They smiled and nodded in response.

Taylor lifted his hand to call for silence, and he quickly got it.

"Listen up. You know who I am and what I'm about. The enemy leader is on Earth and in this very country. I intend to seek him out and end his life, but I need help."

"What can we do?" Doyle quickly asked.

Taylor was glad to see everyone in the room seemed as eager as Doyle was.

"First we remove any enemy presence from the town. That includes freeing Commander Kelly ASAP. Second, we reform the MDF, and third, we take the fight to Erdogan. Are you with me?"

There was universal agreement around the room. He could see they were a people that had given up and accepted their occupiers for good. He had given them a glimmer of hope, but he wasn't sure how fair it was. Though the way he saw it, they either risked their lives with him, or they accepted the end of them if they carried on as they were.

Discussion suddenly filled the room, as more than a dozen people started asking questions and double their number began speculating as to answers.

"Please listen to me!" Taylor boomed.

His voice carried throughout the bar, and all were silenced.

"Firstly, I can't listen to every voice here, and we have to act quickly. So, Doyle, you're going to answer my questions. If anyone has anything to add, put your hand up, and I'll get to you."

He looked to Doyle, and the man shrunk before him with shyness as all eyes turned to him.

"How many UEN soldiers are in town?"

"Uhhh…"

"Keep your answers simple, accurate, and as quick as you can," added Taylor.

"Twelve," he finally replied.

"Twelve, is that all? Are you sure? You didn't sound sure."

He looked around the room, and several nodded in agreement.

"Twelve, Sir, I'm sure. Commander Kelly had me keep constant watch and count all occupying forces. He was very clear about that when this began."

"Okay, so what are their standing orders here, and what sort of rotation do they work?"

"They just guard Commander Kelly's home and stand guard at the landing zone. That's it."

"And what sort of hours?"

"Uhh…eight hour rotation, and only four of them on duty at any time. Two at Commander Kelly's home and two at the landing zone."

"That's it? Twelve soldiers, only four ever on duty, and that is what is keeping you all in your place?"

Another man beside Doyle stepped forward. Taylor didn't recognise him. He was at least ten years older than Doyle and was confident in his posture.

"Colonel Taylor, you have to understand; we aren't kept under control by twelve soldiers. We're kept under control of the threat surrounding us. When the Krys first came here, Commander Kelly tried to fight. We lost twenty-seven of the MDF in that battle and had many more wounded. The twelve soldiers that watch us do just that. How are we supposed to fight against whatever comes at us, should we lift a finger against them?"

Taylor was shocked. He had considered the strife they might have experienced since it had begun.

"Twenty seven?" he asked.

"Yes, Sir, including Major Martinez, and Captain Morris is currently being held in the town prison, but he only tried to bring an end to the bloodshed."

"All good men," Taylor said softly.

He nodded as he thought about it and finally looked up at them all.

"The threat before you is that if you turn against these twelve soldiers, you fear what comes next; the day after, the week after, the month after. What if I told you, there is no month after? When Erdogan has control of the planet, you are finished. You were systematic in bringing about the defeat of his relatives and peers. So forget a week from now, a month from now. We have a small window of opportunity to act, are you with me?"

"Of course," Doyle replied quickly and without doubt.

He looked around to the others who were quickly coming round to Taylor. He took his opportunity to strike a home run.

"So we're gonna take down the fuckers who prey on this town, and then we're going after their leader, you got it?"

He knew he was taking a chance trying to take charge of them, but it was worth a shot, so he continued as if they had already agreed.

"So here's what we're gonna do. These two fine gentlemen, Private Lewis and Corporal Robinson are going to handle the two at the landing zone. Doyle, you will accompany me to Commander Kelly's home where we will get him the hell out of there."

"Take care of? What are we talking about here?" a voice yelled from the back of the room.

Taylor looked for the source but couldn't find it, but he decided to respond quickly either way. He stepped over to the body of the German Corporal he had so recently shot dead.

"The enemy is the enemy, no matter what form they take. This is war, and we will fight it as warriors. Any man or woman without the stomach for this may leave now and go home. Though I would highly recommend you either join the fight, or flee for your lives."

There was silence and nobody moved. They hung on to his every word, and he knew he had them hooked.

"So you have half of the plan. There are six enemy combatants currently off duty. I want volunteers to deal with them. That is, to kill or capture them."

CHAPTER TEN

Taylor took a deep breath. He took a peak around the corner. One of the guards was in a vehicle parked across the road from Kelly's home. It was a two-storey residence and larger than any private accommodation he had seen there so far. He looked back to Doyle who stood beside him.

"Where is the other guard?"

"Inside," he replied.

"Where?"

"Ground floor, always near the door, except for an hourly inspection of the ground and first floor."

Taylor stopped for a moment. He was surprised at Doyle's competent assertions. Doyle still looked like a young man, and it was easy to forget the years of war he had fought through and survived. It was in that moment Mitch realised he hadn't given the man enough credit.

"Do you know the guy in the vehicle?"

"Sure."

"Okay, reckon you can deal with him?"

Doyle knew exactly what he meant, but he had to think about it for moment. It appeared that despite all his years of combat, he had never had to take the life of a human.

"Don't think, do it," Taylor said firmly.

He nodded in agreement, though he still looked shaky, but he had to rely on him. He only had Rains with him, and he knew for a fact that he couldn't handle the job.

"All right, so give us three minutes to get into position, and then you take out the guy in that car, you got me?" he asked Doyle.

The young man agreed. Taylor quickly turned and headed for the back of the house and grabbed Rains to go with him.

"Why the hell are you bringing me along? I fly, and that's it," he complained.

"Times change, and you're needed as well to do… whatever you're needed to do."

"Well, all right then, but I fly well because I've done it a million times. Now how many times have I killed a man?"

"Okay, so focus on what you're good at."

Rains froze in surprise. "What do you mean?"

"You know what you are?" asked Taylor, "A world class distraction. You dress like a hobo, you act like a permanently stoned drug addict, and do nothing better than distract men and women from their post."

Rains was still speechless.

"So use it. You're good at it. You're my distraction. You're an old friend calling in on Kelly. You do that, and I'll do what I'm good at."

"And what's that?"

"Problem solving," he replied with a smile. He led Rains on down the side of the building and around to the rear of the building. As they took a corner, Taylor stopped and checked his watch. It was almost time.

"So here it is. I break the lock on the door. You go in, no weapon in hand. You've just arrived, and you're looking for your old friend, Kelly."

"No weapon? I mean; what do you expect me to do, talk the guy to death?"

Taylor reached up and covered Eddie's mouth. It quickly silenced him.

"No, I expect you to do as I ask. It's one guard, who may or may not be well trained. If he is, then he will treat the first sign of movement with the utmost suspicion, and that is what I am relying on."

"And if he's better than trained, exceptionally trained?"

"Well, then he wouldn't be alone, and he'd expect the first sign of trouble to be just the beginning."

"You're not helping," replied Eddie.

But he went forward as asked anyway. He approached the door as confidently as he could, and with his pistol still holstered inside his jacket. Taylor crept up towards the building a few metres behind and approached the back door from a crouched position. He looked at his watch one last time. There were just twenty seconds left until Doyle was to do what he was asked. Taylor counted it down to ten and then put his pistol against the lock of the door where Rains stood, and pulled the trigger.

A shot burst through the door panel, and Taylor gave it a faint push to pry it open. The gunshot could not go unnoticed, and Rains looked at him to ask 'are you serious?' but Taylor merely pushed him through the doorway.

Taylor rushed in behind him and took up a position beside the cover of the nearest wall. Rains froze just two steps in. They could hear footsteps approaching, and Rains was still frozen. He'd stood beside marines and fought before, but never had he been tossed into such a high stress situation. A moment later, a man rushed towards him with a gun in hand and yelling, "Don't move, do not fucking move!"

The gunman got within a metre of Rains when a shot rang out, and blood spurted out across the floor. The man dropped lifelessly to Rains' feet.

"This is not what I signed up for," Rains stated firmly.

"None of us did," Taylor murmured, as he patted him on the back and stepped on through to the next room. As he did, he was struck in the face with a baseball bat. Taylor stumbled back, and blood flowed from his nose.

He recovered, looked back, and saw Kelly standing in the shadows before them.

"What the hell, Kelly?" Taylor shouted.

The old Commander rushed towards them and grabbed Taylor in shock.

"Mitch? Have you lost your mind?"

Taylor was still reeling from the pain, and blood flowed between his fingers as he cupped his nose.

"Goddamn it, Kelly, you're crazy!"

"Says the man in enemy territory trying to save me. You must have gone out of your mind. Leave now and don't come back."

They all heard a noise from the front of the house and turned to confront it. Taylor held his pistol up with one hand while still holding his bleeding nose with the other, and Kelly defiantly lifted his old school wooden bat. Out of the shadows came Doyle. He was a little shaky and had blood on his collar and hands. Kelly turned to Taylor.

"What have you done?" Kelly asked, horrified.

Doyle shrugged and pointed to Taylor for answers.

"You put him up to this? You've no idea what you've done. You've probably guaranteed our deaths."

"No, that was done the day the UEN took control of this town from you," Taylor answered him quietly.

* * *

Robinson crept up beside a parked car and peered over towards the guard station they had first seen when they arrived. He ducked back down to Lewis.

"We've got to take them down without them getting a signal out."

Lewis nodded in agreement.

"What would get their attention enough that they'd come out but not report in anything suspicious?"

He got no response.

"Wait, I got it. Two drunks shambling over a landing pad start a punch up. How are your acting skills?" he asked with a smile.

Without waiting for a response, he stepped out into the open and began stumbling towards the guard post station. He swayed from side to side as if he would fall over any minute. He turned back to look at Lewis and staggered a metre wide in a massively exaggerated state of intoxication.

"Hey, Lewis, you fucker! Where are you? Lewis!" he screamed.

It was part of the act and meant as an order at the same time. The Private stepped out and followed after him. His feigned drunkenness was about as unconvincing as Robinson had ever seen.

"Every goddamn time you get drunk, and every goddamn time you make it my problem!" he shouted. He spun around to notice he'd just started to get the attention of the guards.

"You gotta learn to handle your drink!" he yelled, as he stumbled back towards Lewis and fell against him.

"Whoa, whatta you doing?" he asked aggressively.

He pushed Lewis, causing them to part.

"Hit me," he whispered.

Lewis was frozen solid.

"Hit me," he said again.

Lewis hesitated, so he went forward instead.

"You know you're nothing but a lazy punk!"

With that, he slapped Lewis across the face, which left him more surprised at the puny strike than the fact he had struck at all.

"What's the matter? You a coward?"

He slapped Lewis again, and this time he seemed to loosen up and get into the act. He suddenly swung for Robinson and clipped him with a solid blow to the chin. He reeled back and exaggerated an almost falling action, as if he'd been hit by a freight train.

"Why, you son of a bitch!"

He rushed back at Lewis and grabbed him in a standing clinch.

"Stay on your feet," he whispered.

They tussled, and each pretended to try and throw the other, punching with hooks and uppercuts. As they turned, they could see the two guards approaching. They kept up the act right until the point they felt the guards grab them and try to tear them apart. They suddenly released their grip, and Robinson turned and struck the first in the face with an elbow, knocking him to the ground with a straight punch to the face as he tried to recover.

Lewis simply grabbed the other guard's pistol from his holster and held it to his stomach, causing him to freeze solid before him.

"You've gotta be the worst actor I've ever seen," joked Robinson to Lewis.

"Yeah, well, it worked, didn't it?"

* * *

Taylor and Kelly sat at his breakfast table. Kelly looked like a broken man, one who had accepted defeat a long time ago.

"So why here, why did you come for me?" he asked.

"Because I need you. I've got one shot at killing Erdogan, the enemy leader. I need help from within this country, and you are all I've got."

Kelly shook his head.

"What?"

"You just don't know when to quit, do you?"

"No, damn right I don't. Quitting ain't in my blood," he quickly snapped, "and I wasn't aware it was in yours either."

"It isn't about quitting."

Kelly tapped a few controls on the table before him, and a large screen projected on the wall. It was a news channel with a female news anchor reporting from the rubble of what could be one of a hundred cities. Text along the screen passed by with all those cities which had fallen to the Krys and their UEN allies.

"Oh, come on, this is just propaganda," added Taylor.

"Yes, but that doesn't make it any less true."

The reporter continued on, "A number of EA leaders have been killed in targeted attacks, and we are already getting reports of evacuations taking place throughout most remaining hold out cities. The grand Lord Erdogan has repeatedly asked us to convey the message that all who lay down their weapons will not be harmed. The war is over. It is time to stop fighting."

Taylor shook his head.

"You don't believe that shit?" he asked Kelly.

"You're damn right I do, and it's time you did as well."

"Even if it were, we can't surrender. There will be no peace with Erdogan."

Kelly nodded in agreement. "Then there remains but one solution."

Taylor thought for a moment.

"You're not suggesting?"

"I am. You once told me to leave my homeland because it was the people who made it home, and that without them none of it was important, did you not?"

Taylor nodded. "But it isn't over. We still have a chance of taking him down."

"Get real, Colonel. You can't take down the most lethal opponent the World has ever known with you and a few old soldiers. This fight is over."

"It can't be over. We've fought too hard. We've sacrificed too much for it to be over."

"And yet you cannot change what is. You can only do the best with what you have."

Taylor was silenced.

"So you're saying what, run? Where? Nowhere on Earth is safe."

"I agree."

It hadn't occurred to him that running meant leaving Earth, but it was clear that was what Kelly was implying.

"We can't. How could we leave?"

"You are facing defeat within what, a few weeks. You've pulled off some miracles before, there is no doubt, but you know this is an impossible situation. So what are your options? Fight on, and die along with your friends. Surrender, and accept the rule of the enemy."

"Never. There is no living in peace with Erdogan. He'd kill us all."

"Then you have the answer. Run and live to fight another day."

"This isn't my decision."

"No, but if I'm thinking it, and you're warming to the

idea, maybe others will too."

Taylor felt sick at the idea. They heard the doors of the house open, and he jumped to his feet and drew out his pistol. But as he took up position behind the counter, Kelly merely sat comfortably where he was. Several figures approached from down the hallway until finally they came into view. Captain Morris was at their head.

"Good to see you again, Colonel," he said in greeting.

Taylor lowered his weapon and took a seat once again. He looked to Morris and Rains.

"Kelly reckons we have no hope but to run, to flee from Earth, what do you think?"

Rains could not help but laugh.

"I'm not sure what's so funny," stated Kelly.

"I'm sorry, but how else can I take it? It's all a joke. We leave this world, then we might as well have given up years ago when this all began."

"No," replied Kelly, "none of your time and efforts was wasted. This war can still be won. The Battle for Earth can still be won. But not now."

"And if we leave, how will we ever be able to come back strong enough?" Taylor asked.

"I don't have all the answers, but I know if we stay, it's over."

Taylor looked back to Rains.

"What do you think?"

"It sucks, but it may be the only option we have out of

a whole list of sucky options."

"Either way, it's not our decision to make," Morris joined in.

"No, if we leave, we have to leave en masse or not at all," replied Kelly.

"How do we do it?"

"First thing is we've got to get back to our own lines. If you're thinking this way, then I bet a good many others are, too. They may just need a final push."

"So we're really doing it?"

"We're gonna try."

"We can't go with you, not yet. No way we'd get across the border. Captain Morris will go with you as my representative. If you get this plan off the ground, we'll join you."

"You'll need a ship, probably several for all your people."

"Don't you worry about us, we can handle ourselves. Just remember, what matters more than anything else is this. People. If we're going to survive this, and stand a chance of winning in the long run, we need people. Not a few hundred or a few thousand. Not even tens of thousands. But millions."

"You're talking a mass exodus?" Rains asked.

"That's exactly what I'm talking about. It's that, or it'll never work."

Taylor took a deep breath and tried to take it all in. He could feel some weight lifting from his shoulders at the prospect of leaving the war behind, the war he now knew they could not win.

"You know if we could just have gotten to Erdogan."

"Then he would have killed you, and you know it. There will be a time to confront him, but it is not now."

Taylor wondered if he had subconsciously gone to Kelly knowing he would be the voice of reason. He was glad he did, but it was still hard to stomach."

"Then that's it. We get back to Dupont, and try and get this through to him."

"You have to. The survival of the human race depends on it."

"When?"

"Now, Rains. We cannot afford to waste any time. Much longer, and we won't have any options left. Kelly, replace the UEN soldiers with your own people and continue on as if nothing happened. Be sure to keep the survivors under lock and key. I wish you every luck."

"And you, too."

With that, he got up and left with Rains and Morris at his side. Doyle turned to leave with them, but Taylor shook his head.

"Your place is here with Kelly. Do your duty," ordered Taylor.

"So that's really the plan?" asked Rains, "Round up the population of the World and head out into space?"

"Those that will come, and something like that, yeah."

"And do what? Head out into the unknown and hope for the best?"

"The unknown is a whole lot better than what we got right now."

"But it's crazy."

"Yep," he simply replied.

Taylor knew he needed a better plan than that. He wished he had Jones at his side to talk to and plan out their course of action. It wasn't long before they were at the landing bays once more and could see some of Kelly's people manning the guard station. Lewis and Robinson were waiting inside with them. They came out to greet Taylor when they saw him coming.

"You get the Commander?"

Taylor nodded.

"And he's gonna help us?"

"He already has. It's a long story. I'll tell you on the way."

"On the way where? Munich?"

Taylor shook his head and led them to the copter.

"This is Captain Morris, previously of the Moon Defence Force. Captain, this is Private Lewis and Corporal Robinson."

"Nice to meet you, Gentlemen," Morris said as they climbed aboard.

They were quickly off the ground, and Taylor had explained the plan in under a minute.

"Back we go again," muttered Lewis.

"Really think we can do this, Sir?" asked Robinson.

"I don't know," he replied with a sigh.

The whole idea seemed impossible to him. The logistics were beyond comprehension, but the alternative was to lose and probably die.

"Border's up ahead," Rains said shortly after.

Not again, thought Taylor.

"Get your gear on. If we gotta jump, I want to be ready for it," he said to the others.

"Captain Morris, you can use Rains' stuff."

"You sure?"

"Hey, I'm here to fly, not fight!"

They quickly strapped into the Reitech suits and sat back down with rifles in hand. Taylor instantly felt his confidence double as he settled into the equipment that had carried him through so many death-defying encounters.

"We're coming up on 'em now!"

"Where the hell did you find this thing, a scrap yard?" Morris asked.

"Pretty much," he replied.

"So what, you're just hoping we can pass through without issue?"

Taylor nodded.

"Great plan."

"Worked the first time."

"They're checking us out!" Rains said.

A moment later, the comms indicator flashed, and a voice came over the speaker.

"Unidentified craft, you are approaching the UEN border. Identify yourself, or you will be considered hostile."

"What? Robinson asked. "They let us in, but won't let us out?"

"They probably logged our entry into UEN territory. Leaving it again to go into a warzone is going to raise suspicions for a civilian craft."

"Might have been an idea to mention that earlier, Eddie," Taylor said quietly.

"Hey, I thought it was obvious."

"What do we do?" Robinson asked.

"Can't turn back, can't run, can't hide," stated Taylor.

"Then answer them, and give them what they want," replied Morris.

Taylor looked to him for clarification. He had no idea what he meant.

"If we're to get across that border, they need to know it is UEN forces aboard."

"But there aren't."

Captain Morris strode up to the cockpit. "Well, that's not entirely true."

"He reached for the intercom button to open a channel, but Rains stopped his hand.

"Let him try," said Taylor.

Rains looked back in surprise.

"Look, we're in deep shit, and none of us have any answers. He can't make this any worse."

Rains pulled his hand away and waited with scepticism to see what words of wonder Morris could use to pull them out of such a sticky situation. The Captain opened a channel, and they all held their breath for a few seconds, waiting for him to speak.

"This is Captain Morris, UEN. Identification, alpha, whiskey, tango, foxtrot, eight, five, three, two, two, one."

"Please await verification."

None of them expected it to work, but they hoped. The response finally came back.

"You're clear to pass, Captain."

The fighter broke off and left them be.

"No way," said Rains, "How in the hell did that work?"

"We're still officially UEN members. The MDF may have been disbanded, but my commission still stands."

"That's a bit of a stretch," Rains grinned.

"Yeah, well, it worked, didn't it?"

Morris took his seat opposite Taylor once more.

"What were the chances of that working?" Taylor asked.

"Do you really want to know?"

Taylor shook his head.

They continued on without further issue. As they made their approach for Meaux from the north, they could see smoke bellowing from parts of the base, and battles still raging on the plains. It was surreal and looked more like a scene from a movie than anything else. They had all been used to being in a battle, not looking onto it from afar.

On approach, they were glad to be noticed this time and asked for identification and guided in to a secure landing zone. It was clear Dupont had wrestled control of the base and the surrounding area back into his hands, but none of them were under any illusions that it wasn't just a short term measure.

Taylor had half expected Dupont to have a greeting party waiting for them to see if he had succeeded in his mission to kill Erdogan. But as they came into land, they could see that despite the number of personnel in the area, none of them were there for them.

"You think the General is gonna be pissed?"

"I couldn't give a damn, Eddie," replied Taylor.

The second they had touched down, Taylor ripped open the door and made a break for Dupont's headquarters, with Morris close beside him. They stepped inside and found Captain Grey and Lieutenant Ota standing with Dupont, discussing enemy positions. He stopped in surprise, for he had not expected to see any of his own people for some time.

"What are you doing here?" Taylor asked.

"Seems you're not the only one who seemingly ignores his orders when he sees fit," replied Dupont.

"Sir, as soon as we found out where you'd gone, the

entire Regiment insisted on following after you. Captain Grey returned to duty as we left and assumed command."

"And you made no attempt to stop the Regiment coming here?"

"No, Sir," he replied curtly.

He couldn't complain. He needed friends right now.

"So you didn't kill Erdogan?" Dupont asked.

"How'd you know that?"

"Come on, Colonel, what do you take me for?"

"It's true. I went for help from Commander Kelly, formerly of the Moon Defence Force, and he opened my eyes a little."

"To what exactly?"

Taylor took in a deep breath because it was hard for him to admit.

"To the fact we have lost Earth, and to continue on fighting is to see the end of us all."

Dupont nodded in agreement, which surprised Taylor.

"You've been thinking the same?"

"Since before you left. I thought we had a chance with you, and it was worth a shot. But I never believed it would ever work."

"Okay. Kelly believes we need to evacuate Earth, and run to fight another day."

He was surprised at Dupont's lack of response, as if it came as no shock to him at all.

"You already had it in mind, didn't you?"

Dupont nodded. "After we narrowly survived the first war, we all knew then that we came close to extinction. A council of key representatives around the World laid out plans for a mass evacuation of the planet."

"And?"

"And certain resources were set aside, plans put into place. Of course, this was before the division of nations we have today. The UEN nations were well involved with these plans."

"Yeah, well, not a lot we can do about that now."

"So tell me about it."

"It's a long story."

"Give me the gist."

Dupont took in a deep breath and looked around his war room. Every single one of the staff was staring at him.

"Follow me," he said to Taylor, "Just you."

The General led him to his private quarters, and he sat down with a groan.

"Review boards were setup to determine how we could leave Earth. How many people we could take, how quickly it could be done, where we would go, and how we could amass the resources to make it happen."

"Okay," replied Taylor.

He was glad to hear a plan was in place, but he was waiting to hear the caveats.

"Evacuating Earth is not like evacuating a city or even

a country. It is an event of unimaginable magnitude. The simple fact is we never had the resources to get everyone out, not even close. Our best estimates showed we could transport fifty million people into space."

"Fifty million? That's a tiny fraction of the World's populace," Taylor replied in shock.

"Yes, and that assumes no variables, such as an aggressive enemy. Many experts estimated that if we tried such as exodus under wartime conditions, as seen in the first war, we could estimate the total number of human beings that would survive and get free of the solar system to be no greater than fifteen million at best."

Taylor's eyes widened at hearing the shocking figures.

"That's...not acceptable."

"You're assuming we have a choice. If we cannot win this war, we must either flee or surrender."

"And if we did surrender? Would the human race survive?"

"Nothing of our experience of the Krys would indicate so. They have sided with some humans so they could win this war, but what do you think will happen once they have control of the planet?"

"So there is no hope?"

"Oh, there is hope, just only for a minority. When these plans were drawn up, they were intended as a means of survival for the human race. That does not in any way attempt to consider the welfare of any individual or collective of people. It's a numbers game, that's all."

"So that's what is being considered?"

Dupont was silent.

"You've already initiated it, haven't you?"

Dupont took in a deep breath. "It has been clear for a couple of days that our chances here were slim."

"And you put this into action, even before you sent me to Munich?"

"Let's get something straight. This is not about my decision, or any other single person. This is a joint programme initiated by surviving governments and their military leaders. I brought you in here to tell you in person because you can already imagine the hysteria it will create."

"Damn right it will."

"And there is nothing we can do about that. The simple aim now is to save as many people as we possibly can."

"And how are we gonna move that sort of number of people?"

"Barges. They have been in construction for several years now at locations all around the World. They are probably the greatest kept secret of our time. Several hundred space worthy transport barges, each with a living capacity of twenty thousand souls."

"How? Where have they been built?"

"Most have been constructed to appear as permanent ground constructions. Many currently have large populations living within them, under the assumption they have been built for such a purpose on Earth."

"And what, we're just expecting to take off and fly off into the distance, just like that?"

"Allied forces will of course provide as much cover to civilian ships as possible to minimise losses. Ultimately, they can only shoot so many of us down once they become swamped."

"That's gambling with millions of lives."

"It's isn't really a gamble when you consider the alternative. I want you to stick around, Taylor. There are still many factors to consider in order to make this operation a success, but you keep it to yourself, okay?"

Dupont got up and led Taylor to the door. Mitch stepped out of the room with a pale distraught face, a fact that did not go unnoticed by Morris and Grey. He carried on past them without a word. Jafar met them as they stepped out of the bunker. He was standing patiently awaiting them. Taylor patted him on the shoulder as he walked past, and the alien turned and continued on beside him.

"I cannot protect you if I do not know where you go," he stated.

Taylor nodded in agreement. "The ship Erdogan came here in. You say it was famed for having jump gate capacity."

"Yes."

"And it was the only known ship of your people to do

so?"

"Yes."

"Why?"

"I do not know."

"But you are sure it is the only one?"

"I believe so."

"What's going on, Colonel?" asked Grey.

He carried on walking without saying a word. He knew Dupont had asked him to keep it all to himself, but he wasn't one for keeping things from those who he depended on to have his back. He shook his head and finally came out with it.

"Follow me, and I'll explain everything, but it ain't pretty."

CHAPTER ELEVEN

"Sure you want to do this?"

Jones looked up and only had to think for a few seconds before he said loudly, "Damn right!"

"Cologne, here we come."

The pilot had been a volunteer, and Jones had not even thought to ask a single thing about young female pilot besides check the name on her uniform; Befort, and her rank Lieutenant. She showed no fear as she guided them down towards a landing zone at an enemy base.

"You know, just because we go in flying a white flag, doesn't mean they'll give us a free pass. They're just as likely to shoot us, Sir," said Private Wood.

"Yeah, maybe, but we can only do what we can do."

"I told you," said Befort, "This is an unarmed liaison ship. They will not fire on us."

As they came into land, they could see a dozen soldiers

239

waiting with weapons in hand.

"Sure about that?" Evans asked, as he looked out through the cockpit.

"What do we do?" asked Wood, "Put our weapons down?"

"No, we came to talk under a white flag, not to surrender. Keep your weapons on you but lowered at all times," replied Jones, "Show no sign of aggression, and know that you cannot fire upon them, no matter what reason you might have. Once the firing starts we're finished, so don't let it begin."

Jones opened the ramp of the ship and stepped out. It was no larger than that Taylor had recently travelled in, the only difference being everything worked on board. He jumped out with empty hands, though still with his sidearm on his thigh. Wood and Evans followed as he asked and kept two paces behind him.

"You have five minutes to say what you have to say, and then you leave!" an officer shouted.

Jones nodded in agreement. *At least they're not shooting us...yet,* he thought.

"I request an audience with General Schulz!" he responded.

"And you are?"

"Captain Charlie Jones, Inter-Allied Regiment!"

The name clearly meant something to the officer, and he turned to a few other soldiers sanding behind him and shared a few words before looking back to Jones.

"You may confer with me. I am Lieutenant..."

The man stopped as he was clearly getting a transmission through a comms device in his helmet. He seemed surprised by what he was hearing, and appeared to argue with whoever was on the line for a moment before going silent and looking back to Jones.

"The General...will be with you momentarily...please stay where you are!"

Jones nodded in agreement. "Thank you, Lieutenant!"

He turned around and looked back at the two Privates behind him. They watched the German forces around them like hawks, although they all knew they were powerless to defend themselves.

"Sure this is a good idea, Sir?" asked Wood.

"Not really, but we'll all out of options."

"Why would he help us, Sir?"

"Because he isn't an evil man, Evans. He's fallen on the wrong side in this fight, but he hasn't always been the enemy."

"You're clutching at straws a bit, aren't you?"

"Oh, yeah," replied Jones without hesitation.

They waited for five minutes without speaking another word. Finally, they could hear a vehicle approaching, and they turned to see an armoured officers' command car rolling towards them.

"Stay where you are, and make no attempt to raise your

weapons!" the Lieutenant said firmly.

The vehicle came to a halt, and Schulz stepped out with two other officers. One was already whispering in his ear before the door of the vehicle was shut, and it was all too clear that the man did not like Jones or his presence. But more than that, he appeared to be underhand and conniving in his actions. Jones could see he would be a thorn in their side.

Schulz had bags under his eyes. His skin was pale and his hair thinner than when they had last met. It wasn't just age that had weathered him; he had the look of a man suffering under a great burden. Jones saluted him as he approached, and Schulz smiled and returned the greeting before coming to a stop before him.

"Captain Jones. I wish we could meet under better circumstances, although I am glad to see you are well."

His voice was friendly and sounded genuine and honest. *This is not a man actively working for the enemy,* Jones thought.

"What can I do for you?" he asked.

It was an odd scenario, as the General appeared to address him as a friend.

"Sir, I am searching for my wife. She was taken by clandestine forces with the UEN from a military hospital in Meaux."

"I am sorry to hear that, Captain. It sounds a most bizarre situation. Are you sure those are the facts?"

"I am," growled Jones, "I saw it with my own eyes."

"I can honestly say that it had nothing to do with those under my command. I would never give such an order, or knowingly let such a thing happen. There are rules in war as there are in peace."

It was the most friendly and amenable Jones had ever seen the General.

"My sympathies, Captain, but I am not sure how I can help."

"Sir, the craft she was taken away on we tracked to this base. From here on, we have no idea where she was taken, but I beg of you to pursue this and find her for me."

One of the officers beside the General leaned in and spoke in his ear. It was the same dubious character Jones had previously disliked. He knew he was going to be a problem from the moment he first saw him. The General began to respond but was interrupted by the man's whispering once more.

"I am sorry, Captain, but we have no records of any such craft having arrived...and there is nothing more I can do."

"Excuse me, Sir, but that's bullshit and you know it. This is your base. This is your army, and this is on your conscience, should you refuse to help."

The man who had been whispering beside the General finally stepped forward. He was in his early forties and slight. He appeared to have an eternal sleazy smile across his face that stank of an untrustworthy character. He wore the uniform of a Major, but he did not carry himself like an officer, more a politician.

"Excuse me, Captain," he interrupted before Schulz could continue, "but the General does not owe you any favours. We are not aware of your wife's location, nor do we have any duty to assist you in finding her. She is, after all, an enemy combatant. In fact, we should rightly have you detained, right now."

Jones was disgusted by his comments.

"You're a wretched excuse for a man," he replied, "We came here under a flag of truce."

"And yet I see no flag," he replied with a wicked smile.

Jones could already tell the situation was going south. The Major was clearly either an alien agent or a heavily indoctrinated sympathiser. Taylor turned his attention back to Schulz, whom he appeared to be making some headway with.

"Sir, I please ask you again. You are the only man I can turn to for help now. Forces within your control are holding my wife or know who is. Will you help me?"

"You have thirty seconds to get back aboard your ship, and get out of here before I have you arrested," the Major replied for him.

Schulz dipped his head in shame. Jones could see he was disillusioned and did not know how to respond to his predicament. Jones had to keep pressing him.

"General, Sir. Will you let this go on, the butchering of

the human race? Will you continue to be controlled by the enemy?"

He knew he was pushing his luck now, but he refused to give up.

"Twenty seconds," the Major continued.

"You know this is not the way. Fighting alongside the Krys and letting them invade and conquer our planet. You have seen what they are capable of."

"Ten seconds, Captain."

The Major looked around and waved his hands to usher the troops in and to raise their weapons, which they did reluctantly.

"You have five seconds, Captain."

Jones could see he wanted nothing more for them to twitch or make a single inclination of resistance.

"Three, two…"

"Stand down!" Schulz suddenly yelled.

The Major was stunned and looked at him with wide eyes.

"Sir, these are enemy combatants. They probably mean to assassinate you and inform the enemy of vital base information."

"Shut up!" he bellowed.

The General seemed to stand a little taller and a regal presence returned to his posture.

"We cannot help these men!" argued the Major, "They should be killed where they stand!" he screamed.

With that, the General pulled out his sidearm and fired a single shot into the man's head that killed him instantly. His body slumped to the floor, and despite the shock of seeing it, not one of the soldiers reacted. He turned around and walked along the line of his own people.

"That man was a spy, an alien agent. We know they're among us. We all have for a long time. It's time we stood up to them and did what's right. Does anyone have a problem with that?"

They shook their heads. He looked to the other officer who had arrived with him, a younger man who looked most shocked by what he had witnessed.

"Lieutenant, find this ship that took Captain Jones' wife. Find out who took her, when they arrived here, and where she is now."

The man nodded uneasily.

"Now!"

The officer snapped into action, rushing back into the vehicle to sit at a console and get to work.

"I thought we were doing the right thing!" Schulz said quietly, "I thought we were doing the best thing for all of us. But the more time goes by, the more the Krys reveal their hand, and I am losing hope for us all."

"It's not too late."

"For what?"

"Join us. What's done is done, but you can put a line in the sand now and bring an end to it."

"Look around you, Captain. This war is soon to be over, what more can I do?"

"It will be over if those of us who should be fighting for humanity give up."

"And what are you doing here? A war is raging out there, and you aren't fighting it."

Jones nodded; he knew it was true.

"I admit this is a selfish act, but you cannot say I have not given it my all. When I get her back, I'll be taking the fight right back to the enemy any way I can."

"And we are not the enemy?"

"You shouldn't be. You can choose not to be."

Schulz thought on it for a moment. Clearly it was something that had been plaguing his mind for some time. The Lieutenant in the vehicle rushed back to the General and showed him details on a Mappad device. Schulz looked pained even as he looked over the information.

"What is it?" insisted Jones.

"Your wife was here, certainly. But no longer."

He took a deep breath.

"Well, where is she?" Jones demanded.

Schulz hesitated for a moment, not that he didn't want to say it, only that he knew it wasn't the answer Jones wanted.

"She's been taken to the Fatihi, Lord Erdogan's personal ship."

"His flag ship?" Jones asked in surprise.

He remembered seeing the vast ship when it first jumped into the system while they fought to disarm the defence grid.

"Why?"

Schulz shrugged. "I have no idea, and I am sorry."

Jones shook his head. "You are on the side of evil here, Sir. There is still time to come back from it, but I pray you do not leave it too late."

The Captain turned and left without another word. He climbed aboard, and nobody said a word until the engines were running and they were lifting off the ground.

"What are you gonna do?"

"Right now, Evans, there's nothing we can do. We get back to Taylor. It looks like our missions just became intertwined."

* * *

Taylor sat in a room with almost a hundred officers. He knew this was it, the final briefing on what they were to undertake. He couldn't believe it had come so soon, and he wondered if any of the others had any inkling as to what was being proposed. The room was quiet as they all waited for Dupont to address them. He was the only general who had held his rank since the previous war, and that made most treat him like the grand leader he was. Taylor had managed to clip two hours sleep in before the gathering of officers, and he felt a new man for it.

Dupont began talking and did not stop for fifteen minutes. In that time, he had explained all he had told Taylor previously, as well as some more filler information. None of it provided anything useful to him. Most of the officers were stunned by what he had to say, but he could also see relief in many faces at the realisation they may both survive and get away from the relentless struggle simultaneously. Finally he asked, "Any Questions?"

"How quickly can we get people aboard these barges?" came the first.

"It is already underway, has been for some time. As well as being used as city block structures, the barges have also been utilised as refugee centres. Those nations I am presently in contact with have on average eighty-five percent capacity."

"So it is already decided who will go?" asked another.

"This isn't a lottery," replied Dupont, "Every soul who is aboard one of these barges when they lift off, as well as any other humans who can get aboard a space bound vessel, will be coming with us. I don't like it, and I don't expect any of you to either. But we have to face up to what is before us. We save as many as we can. Additionally, priority will be given to serving military personnel over civilians. We need every fighter we can possibly get, if we expect to have even the remotest chance of survival."

"And this is your plan, your decision?"

Dupont shook his head. "This was a joint international emergency measure established under the guidance of key military officials and world leaders."

"But you were involved in setting it up?"

"Yes, but let me just say now. I do not have time for a hundred questions. Time is certainly not on our side. This is our plan. If you do not like it, stay on Earth, and I wish you every luck. The exact structure of this operation and your orders is being uploaded to your Mappads as we speak, Operation Angel, the largest exodus of the human race in our history. The first vessels lift off in three hours, as you will see on your Mappads. That is all the time you have. Colonel Taylor and Major Moye, will you please come forward? The rest of you are dismissed!"

The room quickly emptied as the officers studied their Mappads. As they left, Taylor approached the General. He had never heard of Major Moye, but he could see a tall black French officer approaching in parallel with him.

"Take a seat," said Dupont.

"The two of you have been selected for the most important of operations, one which all else depends on."

Great, no pressure, Taylor thought.

"There is no doubt that many millions will get off this planet, no matter how many die during this operation, that much I am certain of. What is uncertain is how we will escape the reach of Erdogan."

Taylor had seen this coming and wondered what great

plan might have been concocted to get past such a glaring weakness in their strategy.

"Erdogan has ships as fast, or more so, than we do. Hence, if we run and he follows, we will likely lose. So it is not enough to get past his fleet, not even enough to temporarily disable it. Neither do we have any means of destroying it. The only option left to us is to put such a great distance between us that we are beyond the enemy's reach."

"Fine words, Sir, but how is that possible?" Taylor asked.

He looked over to the Major and shrugged, but Moye struck a scornful look and turned back to focus on the General. It was obvious he didn't like Taylor one bit.

"Erdogan's ship, that behemoth up there, we know it has the capability of creating a space gateway all on its own. A technology not shared with any other ship in the enemy fleet."

Taylor could already see where he was going, and he didn't like the sound of it.

"Gentlemen, I want you to meet someone."

A doorway opened behind the General, and an alien stepped though, dressed much like Jafar was when they first met - a bodyguard of a Krys Lord. Its armour was ornately decorated, but he appeared to carry no weapons. Taylor launched his chair back as he stood upright and drew his sidearm to quickly train it on the creature.

"What the hell is going on here, Sir?"

"It's okay, Taylor. He's with us," Dupont replied calmly.

Taylor studied the creature's face. It seemed to show no aggression at all, but it appeared to be carefully and intensely studying him.

"He's on our side!" Dupont repeated, "Now put your weapon down!"

"How do we know he's not still working for the enemy?"

"Because your man Jafar approved him!" yelled Dupont, "Now sit down!"

Taylor was surprised and slowly holstered his weapon and did as ordered.

"This is Aysen, and he tells us he owes some kind of blood oath to Jafar. A guarantee of his loyalty to him and us."

"You're sure about this?"

"Do you trust Jafar?" asked Dupont.

"Yes."

"Then I trust Aysen."

Taylor was having difficulty accepting it. It had taken exceptional circumstances and a long time for him to truly accept Jafar as one of them, and he did not like this being thrown into the mix at such a vital moment in all their lives.

"Aysen has given us vital information regarding the layout of Erdogan's ship, which he says is called the Fatihi. He says he can operate the gateway device. Isn't that right?" he added as he looked to the alien looming over them.

"Yes."

Real conversationalist, maybe he is who he says he is, thought Taylor.

"So we're just gonna fly in, open a gateway, have several millions fly through it to god knows where, and then blow Erdogan to hell as we make our getaway?"

"In essence, yes."

"And what stops us from being blown to hell while we try and do this?"

"Many of the alien resources are on Earth at present and will need some time to get airborne. It will be the job of all remaining forces on Earth to stop them. It will be their sacrifice that will see us to safety."

"And getting to Erdogan's ship, the..."

" Fatihi," Moye replied sternly.

"Much of our space fleet was scattered when this attack first began, but most survived. Many came back down to Earth, and many more on the far side of the Moon. At 1600 hours, an attack will begin on the enemy fleet led by the Washington. Aysen has already sabotaged a number of key enemy vessels, which will give us the upper hand for some time as the battle begins. At such time, one thousand men and women under your command, Colonel Taylor, will breach the Fatihi and carry out your operation."

"One thousand, Sir?"

"You will have your own people, as well troops from Major Moye's 11th Parachute Brigade and the British 15th Commando Regiment. Utilising the Mastiff armoured breaching craft, you will board the Fatihi, open a space gateway, and keep it open long enough for us to get the fleet through, then set the gateway reactor to blow and get the hell out of there."

"And Erdogan?"

"He is most likely aboard at present. Should you get the opportunity, you will end his life."

Taylor could not help but laugh.

"I am not sure what there is to find funny about this operation," replied Moye with a straight face.

"It's just, unbelievable," replied Taylor, "It's insane."

"Yes, it is," Dupont added.

Taylor stopped laughing and turned to the General.

"It is as insane as the possibility of the extinction of the human race. We have a chance, not much of one, but we do have a chance at making a new life for our people. It may not be on Earth, but life must go on. This is our only hope. Can I trust in you to give it your all?"

* * *

"Load up! Load up! Let's move!"

They rushed aboard the Mastiffs that were one of the ugliest craft they had ever seen. They were bull-nosed metal boxes, with armour more akin to main battle tanks than transport vessels. They held a hundred men and women each. Taylor locked himself into a position near the front of the personnel bays. They stood upright in the vessel, almost shoulder to shoulder, with just a narrow walkway between each corridor of bays. They truly were crammed in like sardines.

"Looked a lot more spacious on the outside!" Parker shouted.

He looked up and found her braced in opposite him. They had barely spoken more than a few words to each other since crash landing to Earth aboard the Nassau. There had been no time for it, but he could see she was appreciative of the moment they now had.

"You think this can work?" she asked.

"Probably not."

She wasn't sure if he was joking or not, but she smiled anyway and chose not to find out.

Taylor looked around and watched his Company loading up beside him. They showed no fear at all, despite all knowing what they were about to undertake. They were as calm as ever. A line of Reitech shields were stacked further forward of his position just before the breaching doors. He knew he was at the front of the ship, but he could see no cockpit. Then he remembered seeing a small cubicle at the entrance, and he realised the pilot had the best protected position of all.

It wasn't long before the engines fired up, and they were lifting off the ground. He wanted to look out for one last aerial view of France, but even were he not restrained, there was not a single window on the vessel.

"We're on the highway to hell," he whispered.

Parker had heard the words.

"And there ain't no going back," she replied.

Taylor grabbed a wired intercom device beside him and opened a channel on the loudspeaker that ran throughout the ship.

"This is it," he stated, "This could be our last ever mission but accept that if it is, give it your all, and fight like hell. Remember the survival of our race depends on what we do here today. It's been an honour to serve with you all, no matter what. Just one last thing, we're going to the lair of the beast, Erdogan. You see him, you end his life!"

They all nodded in agreement, but there was no cheering and the tone sombre. He began to wonder if he had just seen Earth for the last time, not because he was risking his life, but because they may never return if they survived.

"Just think of all those millions of people about to lift off from Earth. I wonder how many of them have even been told?"

Taylor thought about her comments but he didn't respond. They all knew what the stakes were, and not one of them showed less than their absolute finest determination to get the job done. The time passed quickly as they went through the atmosphere. Taylor was almost in a dream world as he contemplated the inevitable confrontation with Erdogan. He knew it would come one day.

The ship rocked as the first enemy weapon systems began firing on them. A second shot struck a few seconds later, and then a third. They waited and counted the seconds until the next impacts, but after a full minute they had not come. Taylor looked over to Jafar and Aysen, who stood opposite him in hastily repainted armour and a French flag painted on the side of his chest.

"You really did it?" asked Taylor, "You really sabotaged the enemy weapon systems?"

"Of many of their vessels," replied Aysen, "but they will soon recover to full operational capacity."

Maybe we have a chance yet, he thought.

They carried on for almost ten minutes without incident, and he counted every second on the display on his forearm.

"Masks on!" Taylor yelled.

They each hit the controls on their forearms that sealed their suits and lowered the clear screen on their helmets, sealing them against their collars. It was the moment Taylor realised they had been breathing from an air-conditioned artificial source since they boarded.

Have I breathed my last breath of air on Earth?

Taylor was truly fearful that they had reached the end of an era, the end of humanity, as they knew it. The threat of death to himself and those he loved he had grown used to and was all too familiar with. But their hold on Earth was something he had always held on to. It was the reason they fought. It was the only thing he would never give up. And yet now he had set off from the planet, knowing he may never return, even if he did survive.

This fact bothered him more than anything else. The thought of never stepping foot on Earth again was more worrying than facing Erdogan. It was in this moment he overcame his fear of the alien leader.

I will return to Earth, and nothing will stop me, he told himself.

The ships soared towards the Fatihi, passing several dozen enemy vessels en route. Many were powerless or intermittently trying to redirect. Half of them were unable to act. Simultaneously, the allied fleet was descending on the enemy craft. Railguns and missiles fired on the disabled vessels, but they were soon preoccupied with those enemy vessels still active. The fire began to target the Mastiff column once again, and they could do nothing but absorb the fire.

The heavily armoured Mastiffs had no weapons at all. They were nothing more than armoured coffins with a ramming prow. The relentless fire of the enemy finally smashed through the first Mastiff as they were on their descent to the Fatihi. As the next came under fire, two of the allied frigates soared into view and crossed into the line of fire and took the worst of it. They were struck one time after another and kept going despite it.

The two ships were ripped apart as the Mastiffs made the last few hundred metres and themselves plunged through the wrecks of the allied frigates. Mitch knew their own forces would be taking a beating outside, and he was glad his people weren't able to see it. He could see their destruction in his head, and it made him feel sick.

They were just moments from contact with the Fatihi when Taylor locked eye contact with Parker. He didn't say a word, but his expression spoke a thousand words. A tear came to her eye before it dropped down her cheek and onto a smile.

Taylor finally opened his mouth to say something to her but was interrupted by the impact they felt when they burst through the wrecked hulk with little resistance. Another of the Mastiffs blew apart under the weight of dozens of shots from enemy vessels, but it was the last of it. The other eight craft used reverse thrust at the very last moment before plunging into the hull of the Fatihi.

Taylor and his people were rocked by the impact, but the restraining braces they were locked into kept them all in position and without injury. His Mastiff came to an abrupt halt after plunging through three interior walls of the ship. Taylor couldn't believe the Mastiff has stayed in one piece. He had never believed in the design and opposed using them.

Fucking things worked after all, he thought.

The braces holding them in retracted five seconds after they came to a standstill, and it felt good to be released from their hold. Just seconds later, five ramps on either side of the Mastiff opened and dropped down onto the deck of the Fatihi.

Here we go again.

He lifted his rifle, cocked the firing mechanism, and then looked out to his Company. They had not yet moved and were looking to him to take the first step. He could see the worry in their faces. Every other insertion into enemy territory had been followed by immediate and rapid deployment. He went to move but stopped for just a second, realising the fear that overcame those around him. He knew all he could do was lead by example.

"We're here. We're within arm's reach of the asshole that is trying to destroy our world. Let's get this done!"

It was all he could think of to say. With that, he rushed for the nearest ramp and leapt out with fervour.

CHAPTER TWELVE

Jones looked around for some sense of bearing. He'd seen the blueprints provided by Aysen, but he still didn't recognise anything. He lifted his arm to study the info on his Mappad and try and get a sense of their location. Now they were inside the vessel, they weren't getting any live updates on their location, and he had to rely on traditional map reading skills.

"Where the hell are we, Sir?" asked Robinson.

He studied the map a little further.

"I have absolutely no idea."

He pinpointed their current location so that he could at least retrace the distance and direction, and then looked up to the room before them. His Company had taken up defensive positions. They were in a broad circular corridor system that curved around either way. It looked almost like an outer ring corridor system, but he already knew the ship featured concentric circuits throughout.

Jones' attention was immediately drawn to the ceiling as he noticed some movement above him. The roof looked organic and seemed to pulsate like veins. It was not like anything he had seen on a Krys ship before.

"What the hell is that?" asked Robinson.

"It doesn't matter right now," replied Jones.

He had to decide which way to go, but knew that until he had some point of reference, he had no idea which one. He set the countdown on his datapad; thirty minutes, it was all they could afford.

"That way," he pointed.

He went forward and led the way. They got just twenty metres before Mechs appeared ahead of them. Jones did not even break stride. He lifted up his shield and held out his rifle beside it, firing as he went forward. The others joined him, and they cut down three of the creatures with little effort. As they passed over the bodies, the ceiling expanded upwards to what looked like some kind of organic organ with seven outlet pipes feeding out to two corridors.

Jones looked at his map and immediately recognised where they were. It gave him new hope as he correlated it with information Aysen had given him.

"What are you looking for, Sir?" asked Robinson.

Jones didn't respond as he studied the map intently.

"Sir, I thought we were here to buy time and raise hell."

"And that's precisely what we're going to do, Corporal, and we're going to rescue a prisoner in the process."

"That's crazy," added Wood.

The Corporal looked to him for answers as he could see Wood knew to what Jones was referring.

"Sergeant Dubois, the Captains wife. She's being held on board apparently."

"What?" asked Robinson.

"It's true," Jones finally replied, "All evidence we have suggests she is on board. If we survive this, we're leaving the Solar system for good, and I am not leaving her here. I'm gonna do everything in my power to get her back, you got a problem with that?"

Robinson shook his head. "We're with you, Sir. Colonel Taylor saw to our families. Let's now see to yours."

He nodded in appreciation before turning and quickly moving on. "We've got to drop down a few floors. Let's go."

He headed for a ramp, but as they started to descend, Jones began to worry about how little resistance they had faced.

"Where are they?" he asked.

"Who, Sir?"

"The enemy. This is their capitol ship. You know how many thousands crew our flagships? Where the hell are all the crew and marines?"

"Guess we got lucky."

"No chance," he replied.

He hated to be cynical in front of his own people, but he didn't want them getting a false sense of security. They reached the level he was looking for, and as they took a bend, they found what he had been expecting, a wall of Mechs. They carried shields locked together and were advancing shoulder to shoulder the width of the corridor. Jones leapt back as a few pulses rushed towards him.

"Fuck!"

He pulled out a grenade and armed it before tossing it down the corridor. A flash rang out, and he peered around to see the Mech shields locked against the floor, and a blast before them that had done no damage besides burning the surface of the shields.

"We don't have time for this," he muttered.

He looked back at the almost one hundred men and women who lined the corridor and hung on to his every word.

"We're going at em. Keep up the fire, give them everything you got, and do not stop!"

He was confident they knew what to do. He threw another grenade around the corner and immediately stepped out and advanced towards the Mech position, once more locking their shields down to the ground. Robinson launched a second grenade with a good throwing arm. It soared over the shield line just as the first blew.

A second grenade followed it, and two explosions

erupted from behind the enemy. One of the shields, and the creature carrying it, fell lifelessly forward and smashed into the burn marks on the deck. Jones opened fire immediately into the gap and kept going forward. The two lines were advancing relentlessly towards each other now, and gunfire did little as another creature filled the gap. They charged at one another like classical hoplites.

The Mechs stood almost a metre taller than Jones and his paras. As they closed, he leapt upwards, using the power of his suit and all his bodyweight to smash into the top of one of the shields, driving it into the creature's face and causing him to roll over the shield and land amongst the creatures.

There was an immense clash as the ten-metre wide lines hammered into one another and ground to a halt. Jones landed on his feet between the Mechs but felt like a child amongst giants. One swung for him, but he ducked, and the creature's spear delved deep into a Mech behind. He noticed it passed through armour with little resistance, just as their Assegais did.

Down on one knee, he drove his Assegai into his attacker's upper leg, and then withdrew as it as the monster began to collapse towards him. He brushed it off with his shield and a quick turn and went onto the next. As he did, Robinson and two of his own smashed their way in to join him. The Mech shield line was broken, and many behind them were not equipped for close combat.

Jones drove forward and smashed one of the Mechs back until it compressed into those behind it and stopped them bringing their pulse cannons to bear. With his shield pressed high against the creature, he thrust his Assegai beneath it. He stabbed three times through its armour and kept pushing so that the dead body collapsed back against those behind it.

* * *

"Get going," said Taylor.

Jafar and Aysen were wearing the engineers' suits they'd so recently acquired. The bodies of their former owners lay thrown aside behind them. They turned to leave, but Taylor grabbed Jafar again.

"You really know what to do, right?" he asked.

Jafar nodded.

"And our destination?"

"I have been entrusted with making that decision, which I will make alone, and no other shall know until we reach it."

"And you know somewhere worth going?

"Somewhere better than here."

It was good enough for Taylor. He let go of his friend.

"Then good luck."

"And to you," he replied.

They wandered off into the distance. He had no idea

where they were going, or how they were going to achieve it, and that left him feeling helpless. He had gotten so used to being responsible for the success of a mission, and now he was little more than a decoy and protection squad. He looked around to his people, and just as Jones had been, was surprised at the lack of enemy presence.

"We're here to cause some trouble, so let's get to it!" he roared.

He rushed onwards in the opposite direction to Jafar and Aysen. Within twenty metres, he could hear gunfire, and it was a welcome sound. The silence and emptiness they had first found made him suspicious, but now he could hear the fully automatic fire of Reitech rifles. He had no idea who was up ahead, only that they were allies. He had hoped it to be Jones, but as he turned a corner he found British troops. He didn't recognise a single one of them, but they welcomed his arrival. They ushered him onwards to an officer.

"Colonel Taylor," he said to introduce himself.

"Lieutenant Riley, Sir."

"Know how many others made it?"

"At least one of our Mastiffs was destroyed en route, not sure any more of our lot made it."

The British officer spoke so matter-of-factly, as if it were no problem at all.

"You hold here. We're continuing further inwards."

"We haven't got long," he insisted.

"No, but we need to appear to making some determined effort as to not arise suspicions. I am going for Erdogan, and if I stand a single chance of finishing him, I will."

"Nail the bastard," he replied.

Taylor went onwards past the firefight into an open hallway beyond. He had to rush through enemy fire, with his shield held beside him, and hope for the best. They carried on. Parker stayed close beside him all the way. He was running now with a newfound determination. Far from being scared of Erdogan, he sought him out relentlessly.

"Taylor slow down!" Parker shouted.

But he would not listen.

Let's end this now, you fucker, he thought.

After several hundred metres, he stopped on seeing a gleaming light ahead, and the silhouette of Erdogan. He was in a room at the end of the corridor they were in, fifty metres ahead. He stopped and stared at the enemy leader for just a moment, wondering if it really was him.

Or is it another hologram?

He raised his rifle and fired a quick shot. The round struck his armour and ricocheted off. He had not made any attempt to avoid the impact and stood defiantly before them.

"What are you waiting for, Taylor?" Erdogan boomed.

The voice carried down the length of the corridor, all the way to the British Company, and it sent shivers down many spines. It was a powerful voice, and no one was left in any doubts that Erdogan was every bit as terrifying as they had feared.

Taylor felt nothing but a burning desire to stick his Assegai in Erdogan's head. He leapt forward and rushed down the corridor at a sprinting pace.

"No!" Parker screamed.

She ran after him, but he had already gained a good few metres on her. The rest of the Company ran on with her, spurred on by Taylor's battle cry as he stormed onwards. Erdogan did not flinch or make any attempt to move. Taylor dropped his rifle and let it sling by his side as he drew out his Assegai.

This is it. This is my chance, he told himself.

"Wait!" Parker shouted.

He did not slow a single pace and rushed through into the room with Erdogan. As he did, the door behind him sealed shut, and he heard Parker and several others slam into it. He ground to a halt and looked around. It was a translucent barricade that had brought his colleagues to a standstill. He quickly looked back to Erdogan and could see the wicked and terrifying grin on his face.

He seemed to stand just a little taller than Demiran had. His armour was almost form fitting over a tall and muscular physique, and a dark red, almost black cloak stretched down to his feet. His head was completely exposed, and his armour enshrined with so many gleaming jewels and

Krys symbols that he looked more like a ceremonial toy soldier than anything real.

For all of the minimalist and plain armour design of the Mech battle suits, it always amazed him how wildly different their leaders looked. It was as if they were kept at opposite ends of a scale in every sense of the word, just to underline the power balance. Taylor wondered for a moment if Erdogan was just a politician and not a warrior at all. He certainly looked more fantastical than anything he had seen before.

"I told you this day was coming, and yet you seek your death sooner than I had imagined," Erdogan stated calmly.

"I am going to kill you, and I don't see why I should be made to wait."

Taylor looked around the room for any sign of other opponents, but there were none. A large throne of steel lay at the far end of the room, and despite the fact he could see two other entrances, there was no sign of other life in sight. The ceilings were several metres high, and the roof decorated with art. He could make out Mech figures fighting several types of figures that he did not recognise. He could only imagine they were murals of some kind depicting Erdogan's great victories.

The walls were decorated with objects mostly foreign to Taylor, but many were identifiable as weapons. Some of Krys origin, but others looked entirely alien even to their culture. Projectile weapons and hand-to-hand combat weapons of all shapes and sizes were displayed as prized possessions.

"Have you any questions before you die?" Erdogan asked.

Taylor shook his head. "There is nothing else I want from you, besides your life."

Erdogan shrugged.

"Your loss."

With that, an armoured hood arose from behind the alien's head and locked into place one plate after another until it utterly encased his head, and the very centre lit up in a letter T shape. It revealed a translucent section where Taylor could see his eyes and part of his mouth, much like an old hoplite helmet. He pulled out from beneath his cloak a weapon that he had been carrying at his flank. It was almost two metres long and resembled nothing more than an iron pole with a cannon ball attached. Taylor didn't want to imagine what it weighed, as the creature took a firm grasp with both hands.

"I am going to enjoy killing you, Colonel Taylor, before I kill her and your entire race," he said, pointing to Parker.

Taylor looked over to her. She was shooting at the clear screen and the mechanisms around it, but to no avail.

"I only wish this could have lasted longer. You are a puny people that will be ended like all others."

"You want my life? Come and take it!" Taylor shouted.

Erdogan rushed at him. He was a little slower than the

271

lighting fast Demiran, but he came forward with immense power. He swung the giant mace vertically with all his strength as if to flatten Taylor with a single blow. Taylor didn't even try to parry the mighty blow. He turned and leapt aside quickly. The massive iron ball struck the ground where he had been standing and shattered the steel floor, causing it to buckle in a metre radius.

Taylor was shocked by the immense power of the blow, but he did his utmost to hide the fact.

"You're faster than I expected. Good. It would be such a shame for this to be over so soon."

Erdogan rushed forward again and swung a diagonal blow that Taylor was forced to parry. He took it on the shield, and it knocked him several paces to the side. He felt pain surge though the arm that still hadn't fully recovered. He grimaced in agony, and that brought another smile to Erdogan's face.

Taylor looked at his shield to see it had buckled slightly in the centre, and the top and bottom now curved out like a banana. Amazingly, it was still intact, but he knew he couldn't take many more like that. It was time to go on the offensive, and he knew it. He rushed forward and ducked as Erdogan made a rushed swing of the hefty and cumbersome weapon.

Mitch narrowly slipped under the blow and thrust up towards the alien, but he backed off at the last moment and pulled his mace back, catching Taylor's right shoulder blade and launching him forward. He landed face first at the feet of the alien leader.

He turned over to see the mace coming for his head and rolled out of the way just in time, but the huge ball struck the shield and smashed it off his arm, embedding it in the floor. Taylor rolled out of harm's way and back onto his feet. He was shaken by the impact and now felt naked without his shield. All he had left was his speed.

"You must try harder, Colonel. This does not impress me."

"Oh, quit your monologuing. You're goddamn boring me!" he yelled back.

He then took a run at Erdogan and used his boosters to launch up over the weapon and flip up and over, landing with one arm around the creature's neck. He raised his Assegai to thrust down into the collar, but as he did so, the alien reached up and took a firm hold on the Assegai. He pulled the Colonel off and swung around until he could no longer hold on. He was launched through the air and landed hard.

* * *

Jones pulled out his Assegai from a Mech, and it slumped onto his shoulder before sliding down and hitting the floor like a brick. He was looking around frantically now for any sign of Coco.

"Where the hell is she?" he whispered to himself.

He looked at the map on his arm once more.

We're in the right place, so where is she?" he yelled.

As his call rang out, a single Mech took the corner; one of the heavily armoured type that their rifles could barely scratch. He could feel the hatred burning deep inside, and the second he clapped eyes on it rushed forward in anger. The Mech lunged at him with its spear-like weapon, but he nimbly ducked under and passed around its back, leaping up onto its shoulders.

The alien had only just begun to struggle when he delved his Assegai down into its collar and drove it up to the hilt. The Mech collapsed forward with him still on its back. Robinson and the others were still standing in shock from where he had first made his assault against the Mech. He finally looked up at them.

"What are you waiting for? Find her!"

They quickly split up, taking several different forks. Jones passed several laboratories of some kind and empty cells, but found no sign of life.

Come on! Please come on, where are you?

"Sir! Captain Jones!" a voice shouted.

He rushed onwards to the sound of the calling until he reached Wood standing outside a cell. He turned to look in and to his relief saw Coco inside. She was restrained on a tabletop, but she had turned to look at him.

"Coco, are you okay?" he cried.

She nodded but didn't say a word. He raised his rifle and fired two shots at the locked mechanism. He barged through the door with his shield and rushed to her side, but just stopped and stared at her for a moment. She still didn't speak.

"I thought I'd lost you," he said, falling to his knees.

She shook her head. "How did you find me?" she asked and began to sob. He looked down at her restrains. There were some kind of metal clamps around her wrists and ankles, but he could see no release mechanism.

"Don't you worry; I'm getting you out of here."

He stood up, pulled out his Assegai, and cut through each of the bands. He carefully helped her to sit up.

"Sir, we haven't got a lot of time left," said Robinson.

He nodded an acceptance.

"Can you walk?" he asked Coco.

She nodded. "I think so."

Jones hauled her off the table and let her stand on her own two feet. She wobbled for a moment before getting her bearings.

"Where are we?" she asked.

"Aboard the enemy flagship."

"What? How did I get here? And what are you doing here?"

"It doesn't matter. All that matters right now is we have to get the hell off this damn thing." He pulled out his sidearm and thrust it towards her.

"You stick close to my side, okay?"

She looked dazed and utterly confused by the situation, but she took the weapon as Jones whisked her away back the way he had come in. A broad smile stretched across his face as he realised he had achieved what he never thought possible.

We've done it, he told himself.

Coco's rescue wasn't the mission, but it gave him hope they may yet succeed in their endeavours.

* * *

Taylor stood empty handed now. His rifle had been ripped from his side during the fight, and only his sidearm remained. He knew it would do little to Erdogan. He began to circle and keep a keen eye on his opponent, who appeared to be waiting for him to act. As he circled, he looked around at the weapons on the walls around them and finally decided on a metre-long pole with a slightly curved metre-long blade protruding from it. He figured he would try speed against his powerful opponent.

As his fist clenched around the shaft of the weapon and drew it from the wall, the blade lit up and glowed green with electric sparks sizzling around its length. Taylor held it suspiciously at arm's length before deciding it was worth a shot.

"You must know that I am impressed," stated Erdogan,

"As weak as you are, you have been a greater adversary than all those who came before you. For such a weak little being, you have done well. How have you survived this long?"

"Quitting just ain't in my nature," Taylor replied.

He rushed forward and thrust with the fiery blade. Erdogan sidestepped and swung for Taylor. He leapt back out of the way and quickly spun the blade over his head and cut across Erdogan's arm as it passed by. The electrified blade cleanly sliced into the vambrace of his armour.

As the alien Lord took a pace back and lifted his giant mace, he looked at the wound on his arm. The faintest trickled of blue blood seeped from a slash in his armour.

"So you aren't all powerful, after all? You bleed like every one of you I have killed."

"Enough of this playing. It's time to die!"

He rushed forward and swung the mace vertically, causing Taylor to jump aside, but he slammed his body into Mitch and forced him to stagger back across the room. As he tried to get his balance, Erdogan rushed at him, swinging the mace. All he could do was lift his weapon to parry the incoming attack, but it wasn't enough.

The mace struck the pole blade he carried and snapped it in two with little resistance. The mace ball then struck Taylor's armour at his solar plexus and threw him back against a back wall. He felt the wind being pulled out of his lungs, and he was shocked by the sheer power of the alien.

He was starting to realise he may not be able to win, and the desperation of the situation was weighing heavily on him. He reached for the nearest weapon to hand, a two-metre long pole, with a cutting blade and spike at one end resembling a halberd. He went forward and swung with the reach, but it was easily met with a parry from the shaft of Erdogan's mace.

Taylor swung a few more strikes, but he could not get through and was starting to run out of options. He knew in his heart he could never beat any of the alien Lords alone, and yet he had attempted it, anyway. It was starting to sink in now that he may well die there in that room.

Was it all for nothing?

The two of them had parted and stood off several metres from each other now. Erdogan still looked as smug as ever. He knew Taylor couldn't beat him. Taylor looked over to the doorway where Parker and the others were still trying to get through. She stopped and stared at him. She could see the desperation in his face. They both knew he couldn't win.

"This is the end for you, Colonel. Your people cannot escape, and neither can you."

He rushed at Taylor, and despite Taylor cutting in with the halberd Erdogan caught it and drove him up against the sidewall. Taylor was crushed and lifted up off his feet. His weapon was pinned across his body, and he could barely move a single centimetre. Erdogan's helmet retracted back, and his face closed in towards Taylor's.

"Good bye, Colonel."

He drew his body back and kept one hand against Taylor, still pinning him to the wall, and lifted his mace in one hand. It was raised up ready to strike Taylor's head. He knew he couldn't survive the strike. He struggled but could not get free.

It's over, he thought, but he could not let Erdogan have the satisfaction of seeing him look weak.

"You know some day it's gonna be a human who takes your head off!"

Erdogan smiled, lifted the mace a little higher and went to swing it but felt his arm lock. He looked down. Jafar was beside him with a firm grasp on his arm.

"Let him go!" Jafar shouted.

Aysen approached from the other flank to strike, but Erdogan had already seen him. He launched Taylor at Jafar, and the two tumbled over to the floor. He then turned on Aysen. He took a swing, and Aysen barely ducked under, rolling out of the way across the room.

Taylor was quickly on his feet, but they were all frozen like statues. Erdogan stood at one wall with all three of them in front of him. He looked completely unfazed by their presence.

"Great timing," Taylor said.

"We do not have much time," Jafar replied.

Taylor looked down at his datapad, and as his eyes met with Erdogan, he could see some confusion in the alien's face. He was trying to comprehend what they meant.

"You thought we came here for you, jackass?" Taylor asked.

He laughed as Erdogan's face turned to stone and then disgust.

"Whatever plan you have, it will fail," he replied.

But Taylor continued to smile, seeing the doubt in his face. Jafar drew out a two-handed sword, and Aysen took out a long blade spear. Taylor raised his halberd up one last time.

"So how about it? Let's dance."

Erdogan rushed right for him, and with the weight of a massive strike snapped the Halberd in two as Taylor lifted it to parry. He came in with another strike, but Aysen lunged at him, driving him back. Jafar cut towards him. The sword cut into the pauldron of his armour, but he backed off before it could penetrate deeper.

Aysen was the first to go forward and thrust repeatedly at Erdogan. He dodged and brushed off the spear thrusts with his arm, until finally closing and striking Aysen with a punch to the face that landed him flat on his back. Jafar was next and cut in with his sword, but Erdogan parried both attacks with his mace and then slid the ball end forward into Jafar's face. The blow knocked him back several paces, and blood gushed from his nose.

Taylor looked to his friend in surprise. He could not believe the power and speed of Erdogan and was beginning to wonder if even together they stood any chance at all. They went at him again with another determined attempt while Aysen was still on the floor. Taylor leapt upwards and drove the counterweight of his halberd at Erdogan. It knocked him back a little, and then he swung the halberd blade over in a massive arc, which he didn't believe anyone could parry.

Just as it was about to connect with Erdogan's head, he raised his mace and parried with arms at each end of the shaft. The halberd stopped dead with the blade just centimetres from the alien's exposed head.

"Nice try," he replied.

With the halberd blade locked over the mace, he pulled it forward and ripped the weapon from Taylor's grasp. Jafar jumped in quickly as Taylor was left helpless. His cut was parried, and he closed with Erdogan and reached under to grapple but was struck on the back of the head with the mace grip. He fell face first to the floor.

"Look at you, pathetic!" he sneered.

Taylor could see Aysen crawl up onto the throne and touch a few buttons on a control panel on one of the arms while Erdogan's attention was focused on him. They were all beaten and bloody and could see no way of winning, let alone surviving. Suddenly, Aysen gave out a deafening cry as he charged towards Erdogan and crashed into him, driving him through one of the other doorways. As they passed through, the door sealed and locked shut behind them.

"What the hell is he doing?"

"Saving us," replied Jafar.

"What? No!"

"Come on, we have to leave."

"Not without him."

"He did this for us. Now honour him and live."

Taylor looked at Parker; still staring at him from behind the doorway he had first entered. She looked so utterly relieved.

"Get to the ships. We'll meet you there!" he shouted to her.

CHAPTER THIRTEEN

"He did that for you?" Taylor asked as they rushed through empty corridors to find their way back. He had nothing but his sidearm in hand and prayed they would not meet any Mechs.

"Yes, he owed me a great debt. One he has now paid."

"He knew we couldn't win?"

"Yes," Jafar replied.

"You knew we could not beat him?"

"Erdogan is the most dangerous of my people to ever live in many generations."

"So that's a no?"

Jafar didn't respond. It was a terrifying thought to know that one day he would surely have to face Erdogan once again. Taylor had never felt so outclassed by any opponent in his life, and he had fought some of the best.

"Next time we face him, we go in prepared and able to

win," he added.

They carried on room after room and corridor after corridor. Jafar seemed to know where he was going, and Taylor simply had to trust him. Finally, to his surprise they reached some of their Company and the Mastiff they had come in on. Parker rushed up to him and wrapped her arms around him, but as he held her firmly, he noticed Jones over her shoulder.

"What are you doing here?" he asked as he let her go. Then he noticed Coco standing with him.

"Well, I'll be damned," he added.

"Good to see you, too, Colonel," she replied.

"Our boat is totally out of action. We aren't getting out that way," said Jones.

Taylor saw they hadn't taken many casualties and so could already tell they weren't going to be able to fit everyone aboard.

"You send out a pick-up beacon?" he asked.

"Yes, we're awaiting pick-up."

Taylor looked down at the watch on his datapad.

"Jesus, we're cutting it a bit fine."

"Time you head off. We'll wait for the boat."

Taylor didn't want to agree, but he knew there was little more he could do.

"We can cram in about forty of your people. It won't be comfy, but it's a start."

"Much appreciated, and I would ask that you please

take my wife with you."

"No, I will stay with you," she insisted.

Taylor could see the concern in her face, but he could also see the determination in Jones'. One way or the other, she was going with him.

"Please no," she pleaded, "I just got you back. I can't lose you again."

"Exactly my thoughts," he replied, "Now, we will get off this boat, but I want to know my wife and son are safe at the first opportunity. We may have to go out into the black to get a lift, and you don't even have the gear. I need to know you are safe, and I don't have to worry about you any longer. You are going with the Colonel. You will be safe with him."

She opened her mouth to protest but could see in his eyes that it was no good. Finally, as a tear dropped down her cheek, she nodded in acceptance. He turned around to Taylor.

"Get her to safety, both of them, you promise me?"

He looked deadly serious. Taylor stretched out his hand in friendship to confirm it, and Jones took it.

"She will make it. You have my word."

He looked at his datapad once more before looking to the others who eagerly awaited his word.

"Let's load up. We're out of here!"

Cheers rang out as they rushed aboard the Mastiff.

"You know you look like hell, Mitch," Jones joked.

He nodded in agreement.

"So did you get him?"

Taylor shook his head.

"Losing your edge?"

Taylor smiled. He leaned in close.

"Erdogan is like nothing we have ever seen or faced. You get your ass off this hulking piece of shit ASAP, you hear?"

Jones was surprised at how defeated Taylor looked, and he was starting to understand how serious their situation was.

"We're about to enter a new phase in the history of humanity, and I want you there for it," he added.

He turned, took hold of Coco, and led her into the Mastiff. She pulled free and looked back one last time, blowing a kiss to Jones as she continued to weep. Taylor pulled her along once again inside the ship. He put her into one of the bays and strapped her in before heading back to the pilot's cabin.

"We ready to go?"

"Yes, Sir."

"Then take us out."

"Aye, aye, Sir."

Taylor looked around to see the pilot flew via a series of cameras that showed all angles of the exterior of the bullish craft. He fired up the engines as the doors sealed shut. They were crammed shoulder to shoulder throughout. A few moments later, they lifted off from the deck and soared out through the gaping hole they had created.

"Any news on the fleet?"

"Yes, Sir, whatever that alien did to interfere with the enemy systems, we have regained full communications."

"And how are they doing?"

He did not respond.

"Well, come on, tell me."

As they broke free of the enemy vessel, he could see some of the extent of it to himself. There were floating hulks of vessels all around of both human and alien construction. A few battles still raged between those craft still able to fight, and he could see several hundred vessels approaching from Earth's atmosphere.

"Is that all that made it?" he asked in horror.

The pilot nodded. Taylor shook his head. There was nothing he could do about it now; just hope Jafar and Aysen's efforts had worked. He looked at Earth and was simply in awe of its beauty, despite all of the horror going on at ground level. From space, it looked picturesque.

"Are we really leaving?" the pilot asked.

"Leaving or dying," he replied.

He looked up to Parker.

"Get Dubois a suit."

"Will she need it?"

"No idea, but let's play it safe."

"How long?" he asked Jafar.

"Any moment now."

Taylor took a deep breath as he prayed for the plan to work. He closed his eyes and looked away.

"Sir, I'm getting some readings... what the hell is that?"

A beam of light ten metres wide surged from Erdogan's ship. He looked up in time to see it. For a moment, they all thought it was a weapon. But the light stopped and expanded out into a huge sphere that began to spin. It looked just like the entrance of a space gateway, only without the framework.

"Have you done it, is that it?" he asked Jafar.

Jafar nodded.

"That's it. We've got a way out of here!"

A few cheered, but most realised that survival meant leaving Earth, and that was a terrifying thought. He tapped his communicator.

"Jones, come in, Jones."

"Colonel? What's happening?"

"We've got our way out of here. What's the ETA on your ride?"

"Gunboat just offered us a ride. It's en route."

"Good, get the hell out of there now. We're getting out of here."

"Affirmative, over and out."

Jones looked back to those who remained with him. Five of them were firing back down a hallway at Mechs advancing on them. The rest eagerly looked to him for the order to leave.

"That's it. Boat is incoming, but we can't get aboard. We're making a jump for it. Let's go!"

None of them moved, as they couldn't believe the time had finally come.

"Come on, go!"

They rushed several rooms over to the breach and looked out to space. They saw the ship approaching. A fast and agile gunship with limited stowage capacity.

"It'll have to do," he said. He took the leap and used his boosters to accelerate towards the incoming vessel, which banked and came to a standstill ready for them.

As he floated through space, he looked at Earth just as Taylor had and marvelled at its beauty. "It was worth fighting for, wasn't it?" he asked through his intercom. Nobody responded, but he knew they felt it too. The large side door opened on the gunboat ahead, and Jones was first through and turned to wait at the door to see everyone safely aboard.

"Come on, come on! Come on!"

The last of them was through. He hit the door shut button and felt the artificial gravity systems take effect. He rushed through onto the bridge to find the Captain awaiting him.

"Glad to give you a ride, Captain Jones."

"Much appreciated. Now let's get a move on."

"With pleasure."

He looked out to see the fleet approaching the jump gate.

"It's really happening? We really did it?"

Pulses and missiles continued to race before them as the two sides continued to duke it out. He could see the Mastiffs towards the rear of the fleet, but they were a distance off.

* * *

"We've got incoming!"

Taylor looked at the scanners at a single craft soaring towards them. It was small for a Mech craft, not a lot bigger than the Mastiff they were flying aboard.

"They're not firing on us?" asked the pilot in surprise.

"No," Taylor replied, "They mean to board us."

"What? Why?"

"Because they value whatever we have aboard more alive than dead."

"What, you?"

Taylor shrugged.

"It doesn't matter, but count yourself lucky. They shoot us out of the sky, and we're finished. They board us, and they got a hundred plus angry marines ready to kick some ass."

The ship rocked as they felt the enemy vessel crash into

them from above and then clamp onto their hull.

"All right, let's great ready to deal some pain!"

He grabbed a rifle from a rack nearby and holstered an Assegai from the same source. It felt good to know he was once more facing an enemy he knew he could beat. He knew now that were he ever to face Erdogan again, he had to be a lot smarter about it, but right now, he was happy to take an easy fight.

Sparks flew from the ceiling above, and they parted out as much as they could, waiting with rifles held at the ready. Taylor grabbed a shield from the rack and waited, now still and calm. Twenty seconds was all it took them to cut through the upper hull, and a two-metre square section of the hull collapsed down and landed between them.

All was silent for a moment until a small metal object dropped through the breach.

"Grenade!" Parker shouted.

They ducked for cover, and Taylor looked away and sheltered behind his shield. The cabin lit up with a blinding flash, and their shields only provided a little cover. Taylor was slightly disorientated, but he had been saved from the worst of it. He was quickly up on his feet in time to see the first Mech descend through the hole and land in the middle of them.

There was no safe way to use projectile weapons and so dropped his rifle and advanced on the first creature, drawing out his Assegai. It carried close quarter weaponry as he was now becoming familiar with.

"Come on, you bastard!" he yelled.

He slammed into the Mech with his shield and drove it back against several of his comrades, who stabbed it in the back. It dropped dead without him having to do a thing. He turned around to see another Mech descend into their Mastiff, and one after the other they dropped in.

It was a futile attack, for the weight of numbers aboard the Mastiff swamped the attackers, and it was a killing frenzy. Within a minute, Taylor was coated in blue blood, and he was fully indulging in the pain and suffering he could inflict. It felt good to be winning once again.

Over twenty Mechs had fallen to the bloodthirsty forces of Taylor and his Inter-Allied when finally they stopped coming. Taylor climbed up on to the pile of Mech bodies and stood below the centre of the breach.

"Is that all you've got!" he screamed.

No response came. Then finally the clamps of the ship above began to release. Taylor pulled out a grenade and armed it before launching it up through the breaching door way. They saw a flash above them; the grenade blew just seconds after they had broken loose.

"That's right, that's what you get!" he screamed again.

He looked over to Parker and could see she did not share his faith.

"You're not invincible," she said.

"We're the Immortals, and we always will be!" he yelled

for all to hear.

A few of the marines around him placed sealing pods over the breach that rapidly plugged the hull. But as they did, they felt the ship rock. A pulse had struck it. The flood of excitement vanished when they realised how vulnerable they were. Another two impacts rocked the ship but seemed to have no effect. The Mastiffs were tough, but they all knew they could only take so much.

Taylor rushed over to the pilot to look out across his viewing screens.

"I thought they wanted you alive?" he asked.

"Yeah, well, we just proved to them that ain't gonna happen. Guess they reverted to plan B. How long till we reach the gateway?"

"Three minutes, Sir."

"That's a long time to be taking such a beating."

He looked on the screens at a dozen alien craft on their tail. One of them blew up without warning.

"What the hell was that?" Taylor asked.

"Looks like our guardian angel," replied the pilot.

* * *

"Come on, take them out!" Jones hollered.

They were hot on the tail of the craft chasing Taylor's Mastiff.

"We're running low on ammunition," the ship's Captain

said to Jones quietly.

"This is all you got?"

"We've been fighting since this began. We're the only ones left out of a squadron of five. I know you've been fighting hard, but so have we."

Jones was sympathetic, but he looked back to the screens and saw enemy pulses pounding the Mastiff. They fired a burst of cannon fire and launched missile after missile, which knocked out six of the Mech ships, but as they targeted the last of them, gunfire strafed their vessel. Jones was thrown onto his back and many of the standing crew were launched across the bridge. The Captain was thrown against a console, and his head cracked on the edge. He was briefly knocked unconscious with a deep bleeding cut across his forehead. Warning lights flashed, and a fire broke out on the bridge.

The crew quickly contained it, but the Captain looked to Jones in horror.

"Weapon systems down, and we've got multiple hull breaches. We're losing fuel. We've got power for now and that's it," said the pilot.

"How long until we get to the gateway?"

"Two minutes, Sir!"

"Get me a direct line to that Mastiff!"

Sparks flew out from many of the consoles, and they could all see they couldn't take much more. Another pulse struck the hull and blew a hole through. The pulse struck three British paras and killed them instantly. Another pulse tore a hole in the far side of the hull.

"We can't survive going through the gateway, can we?" Jones asked.

The pilot looked around and shook her head, "I don't believe so, Sir."

"Get me a link with that ship!"

A moment later Taylor appeared before him.

"Good you're okay, Charlie."

"Yeah, sort of, you?"

"We just need you to keep doing what you're doing. You're the only thing cutting us a path to the gateway."

Jones dipped his head.

"What is it?"

"Weapon systems are down, and we've got multiple breaches."

Taylor was knocked aside from several more pulses striking their ship and almost lost his footing. Jones looked out of the cockpit. There was just one Mech ship firing on the Mastiff.

"What are you saying, Charlie?"

"We can't make it, but you can."

Taylor looked stunned. It was the worst thing he had heard in years. His stomach churned, and he felt worse than he had at the prospect of death at the hands of Erdogan.

"No, don't tell me that! You're gonna make it."

"We're out of time, Mitch. You're out of time. You can't take much more of this."

Jones looked over to the pilot.

"Put us on a collision course. All power to the engines, and give us everything you've got."

The pilot wept but did not argue. They all knew they had no chance left anymore.

"Changing course, all power to engines. We're gonna nail these sons of bitches, Sir."

"Don't do this, Charlie."

He was close to tears himself. "I've lost too many friends since this began. Don't let me lose you."

"Twenty seconds to impact, Sir," said the pilot.

The gunfire continued to smash into the Mastiff.

"We can take it. Don't you worry about us," added Taylor.

Coco had heard his desperate words and appeared beside the Colonel.

"What are you doing?" she pleaded.

"I need you and our son to live. I need you all to live. This is the end for me, but you can keep on living for us all. I love you Coco. And Mitch, you better look after her, you hear?"

Taylor nodded in agreement, but Coco collapsed into tears. They all wanted just a few more seconds to say a few more words, but there was no time left. The gunship plunged into the Mech craft and vanished in an explosion that erupted as the two collided.

The screen Taylor and Coco were watching went black. They were speechless as they were left in horror. Neither of them could believe what they had just seen. She collapsed into his shoulder, and he could do nothing but wrap his arms around her as she shook from crying. He couldn't find a single word of comfort, as he could find none to console himself.

Taylor looked up. Parker was staring the two of them. She had been there the whole time and shook her head in disbelief. A few moments later the screens flashed with bright light as they entered the gateway. They knew they had made it now, but they could feel little relief as their hearts sank at their losses.

The journey through the gateway wasn't long at all, but it felt like a lifetime as they licked their wounds. Coco didn't let go of Taylor the whole time. Finally, they came out the other side, and the screens returned to normal. Once more they could see the blackness of space and the fleet before them.

The gateway closed behind them, but they could see three Mech ships on a direct collision course with the Washington. The flagship was still burning and had been badly beaten in the battle. Taylor looked at the enemy vessels and forgot Jones for a moment.

"Set a course for the Washington. Get us there now!"

The pilot did not hesitate. The enemy vessels plunged

into the Washington, barely slowing down.

"We can't fight every battle," Parker said.

"No, Eli, but look at them. A couple of hundred ships left to fight for the human race. That's it. That's all we saved. Now we have to protect what is left."

They raced for the Washington and were less than a minute behind the Mech invaders.

"Put us in right here," said Taylor, pointing to a particular area on the ship.

"What, why?" asked the pilot.

"Quickest way to the bridge. It'll be where they're heading."

The pilot asked no more questions. Taylor looked down for a moment at Parker. She was now comforting Dubois, and he was appreciative of the fact.

"You look after her, you hear?"

"We can't stay here. It won't be safe."

"No, you're coming with us all the way. You just stay safe."

She knew he was showing concern more for Dubois than her, and agreed as a result. The pilot brought them up alongside an access door of the Washington, and Taylor opened the doors leading to the entry point,

"We haven't got access codes, have we?" Silva asked.

"Access codes?" Taylor asked, almost raising a smile.

He pulled the pin on two grenades and dropped them down the boarding tunnel. An explosion rang out, and without even checking, he leapt out and into the tunnel. He didn't say a word to the others, knowing he didn't need to. A hundred and thirty Inter-Allied personnel were at his back, and he was more determined than ever.

When he went after Erdogan, he was fighting for himself; now he was fighting for the survival of the human race. He knew the ship's layout well, after having spent plenty of time aboard, and led the boarding team quickly towards the bridge.

"Did we really just do this?" asked Silva, "Jump into an unknown system?"

"Unknown, but a damn sight safer than where we came from."

It was hard to disagree.

They heard gunfire and screaming up ahead, and Taylor knew they had come to the right place. He did not slow down nor show any caution. He advanced with determination and his shield held before him. He took a turn into the main access corridor to the bridge and found himself facing the backs of a dozen Mechs. Taylor squeezed the trigger on his rifle and kept it down as he advanced and strafed the Mechs.

Eight were cut down by the time his magazine ran dry, but he did not stop. Taylor rushed for them and drew his Assegai. He leapt at the first one, crushing its own weapon against its body with his shield. Taylor drove his weapon deep into the creature's chest. Without breaking stride, he continued on, spun under a Mech's pulse cannon, and stabbed to the leg. He drew the Assegai out and thrust it through the armoured faceplate as it keeled over.

Silva rushed the other Mech beside him and stabbed it a half dozen times. By the time he had finished, Taylor's Assegai lay embedded in the final creature. Still he did not stop. He strode aboard the bridge, finding many of the crew huddled inside with small arms. They looked terrified.

"Who is in charge here?" he yelled.

Admiral Huber stepped up from behind the operations table.

"Well, well, Colonel Taylor. This is no surprise at all. The whole World falls apart, but somehow it's always you still standing. Thank you."

Jafar and Silva paced in beside him. Taylor turned back to them.

"Organise hunting parties to sweep the vessel and assist the marines aboard."

Silva acknowledged, rushing off to carry out the orders. Taylor turned back to see Huber was still stunned.

"So, you are in charge of this fleet still?"

He nodded.

"Then I guess you are humanity's new leader. All of our lives are in your hands."

It was a lot to take on board, and Taylor couldn't believe he was even saying it. He stepped up closer to Huber.

"Are we safe?" he asked.

"What do you mean?"

"Are we safe? Any sign of Mech forces in the system?"

"I don't know. We haven't had time to check."

Taylor waited for him to do so. He turned around to the crew. "Get a display of the surrounding area up, and let's see what we're dealing with."

The whole bridge lit up, becoming a giant 3d display screen. Several planets could be seen before them and a number of moons.

"And what are our numbers, Admiral?"

"Ships?"

"People," Taylor answered him, "This isn't about fighting personnel. It's about people, so how many did we save?"

Huber turned to his ensign.

"I want reports from all ships immediately...number of souls aboard."

The ensign relayed the command, and they all stood and waited. It took almost fifteen minutes for the reports to come in, and they remained mostly silent until that time. Huber looked at the report and ushered Taylor over to see it too.

"You need to address the fleet," he whispered to Huber.

The Admiral looked surprised. Addressing civilians was an alien concept to him.

"Sir, this is the human race now. They need leadership.

They need hope."

Huber opened a channel to the fleet.

"This is Admiral Huber, commander of the fleet...I...I...I want to commend you all. You have made it. We have made it. Initial reports suggest we number three million souls across two hundred and eight vessels. This was our mission, and what I can tell you is, mission successful!"

Cheers rang out from the bridge crew, but Taylor could not join in. He had lost too much to feel any sense of hope. Huber looked to him for answers, and he only glared back. It was Huber's job now, and he knew it. He went back to the comms to address the millions of humans now clinging to his every word.

"We are three million. We are the survivors. We are the resistance! Together we will continue onwards. Hope, hope is what we have now. Remember that."

He ended the transmission, for he was at a loss for words.

"Well done," Taylor said.

"I'm not the man for this," he pleaded, his voice barely audible.

"You are our leader now, Admiral. None of us ever could have seen or wanted this, but we do what we have to do. I have faith in you."

He tapped the Admiral on the shoulder and walked off the bridge. As he reached the corridor outside, he found Parker and Dubois sitting amongst the dead Mechs. Parker appeared relieved and joyous that they had both survived, but Dubois looked like she'd just lost everything in her life. Taylor knelt down beside her.

"Sergeant Dubois...Coco."

She looked up to him.

"He did this for all of us, didn't he?"

"Yes. Charlie Jones was the finest man I ever knew, and will remain so in our memories. We have survived to tell his story, and you have survived. You are the future. You are carrying his child, the child of Charlie Jones and Coco Dubois. Just imagine what a soldier he will make."

She looked horrified.

"No, not a soldier, never a soldier."

Taylor remained silent, for he knew he would win her over yet. He knew any child of Jones could be nothing but a fighter. He stooped in closer and embraced her like a sister. He couldn't yet come to terms with the loss of Charlie, but it gave him hope that there would be another Jones.

He got back up and strode onto the bridge. "I want to address the fleet," he stated.

Huber didn't know how to take it, so simply agreed. Taylor's presence was terrifying. He was coated in blood and dirt, and his reputation was well beyond celebrity status. Huber opened a channel.

"This is the Admiral speaking. I have here with me Colonel Taylor of the Inter-Allied Regiment. The

Immortals. He's asked to speak a few words, but first I would like to personally thank him for his efforts. Colonel, please go on."

Taylor took a deep breath. He couldn't believe what had happened in so few days. They had seemingly been sure footed on Earth one morning and in another star system by the end of the day.

Where the hell do we go from here? he asked himself, but he knew he couldn't show so much doubt and fear to those who relied on him.

"This sucks. You know it does. I know it does. But suck it up. This is the life we have been given. It is our duty now to protect the human existence. The enemy threw everything they had at us, and yet here we are, still here. Earth is our world, and let me promise you, we will take it back. Remember that. Everything we do from now on is to get our homes back. Fight for it. Fight with everything you have got."

His voice faltered slightly, but then he spoke with clarity and conviction, remembering all those they had lost.

"There is hope. There is always hope."